VOWS
ON ICE

VOWS
ON ICE

BOYS OF WINTER #6

S.R. GREY

Vows on Ice (Boys of Winter #6)
Copyright © 2018 by S.R. Grey

ISBN-10: 1-7325458-1-2
ISBN-13: 978-7325458-1-6

Editing: Hot Tree Editing
Proofreading: Deaton Author Services
Cover Design: Najla Qamber
Interior Design and Formatting: by:
www.emtippettsbookdesigns.com

OTHER BOOKS BY
S.R. GREY

Boys of Winter series
Destiny on Ice
Resistance on Ice
Complications on Ice
Caution on Ice
Player on Ice

Judge Me Not series
I Stand Before You
Never Doubt Me
Just Let Me Love You
The After of Us

Inevitability duology
Inevitable Detour
Inevitable Circumstances

Promises series
Tomorrow's Lies
Today's Promises

A Harbour Falls Mystery trilogy
Harbour Falls
Willow Point
Wickingham Way

Laid Bare novella series
Exposed: Laid Bare 1
Unveiled: Laid Bare 2
Spellbound: Laid Bare 3
Sacrifice: Laid Bare 4

YOU'RE SQUEEZING IT TOO HARD, DUDE!

BRENT

"**F**or fuck's sake, quit squeezing so damn hard, dude."

"Then make it stop moving around so much, Brent."

"I can't. It has a mind of its own. You know that."

Nolan Solvenson, my best friend and teammate on the Las Vegas Wolves hockey team, huffs.

Shit, it looks like he's about to give up.

But he can't do that.

The real fun is just beginning.

I relax my body and lean back in the canoe we're in. Maybe if I lighten up, he'll do the same.

With my newly adopted kicked-back position, and with a

much more positive attitude, I say, "Of course, it's going to twitch and squirm, Nolan. You can't hold it in a damn death grip. Just grasp it firmly and confidently, my man."

Nolan readjusts his hand, grumbling the whole time.

"Okay, okay, but I'm telling you that's what I've been doing."

"No, it's not," I counter calmly. "Just look at how the tip is all plumped up over the top of your hand."

Observing what I'm referring to, Nolan relaxes his grip. "Crap. You're right. Sorry, man."

"Ahh," I murmur, "that's much, much better. You're finally getting the hang of it."

Rolling his russet brown eyes, clearly in irritation, he retorts, "Hey, I think I'm doing a damn good job, all things considered. This *is* my first time trying this, you know."

"I know, I know," I reply as he begins to concentrate more intently on his task.

I know I've lost him for a while. Nolan is like this with everything he does. He's truly a perfectionist.

I guess I am too, in a lot of ways.

That's what makes us such good hockey players and really great linemates. See, I'm the top line center with the Las Vegas Wolves, and Nolan plays on my right wing. That's our line, along with left winger Benny Perry.

Together, the three of us score a lot of goals…and have even more fun.

Though I have to say, I've never had fun quite like *this* before with Nolan.

Ah, there's a first time for everything, though, right?

Quietly, I watch Nolan as he finally gets the hang of what he needs to do in order to succeed at this endeavor.

Finally, I murmur, "Mmm, you're doing a fabulous job now."

"Thanks, Oliver."

Crap, he sounds dejected. I better throw him a bone, offer up some kind of support, or he may give up.

"Hey," I begin with my tempo and tone upbeat, "just remember you already caught one fish so far today. And really, who knows? Maybe there is something to be said for using worms practically smooshed to death as bait."

"Ha-ha," Nolan deadpans since that's what he's been doing. "You're a real funny guy, Oliver. I'm just following through on what you told me to try."

"Sure. Whatever you say," I mutter, chuckling.

Eh, it doesn't matter. Despite Nolan's heavy-handed method of baiting his hook, aka smashing the worms in the process, he's had success fishing at my Minnesota lake house property this morning.

He's never done this before in his entire life, so hooking even one fish is something to be proud of.

Wait, what did you think we were doing?

Perverts!

Nolan garners my attention when he hisses, "Yes!"

He's finally threaded a second nearly squeezed-to-death worm onto his hook. He baited his first line all by himself, as well, which was, surprisingly, the one that landed him a twenty-inch walleye.

Too bad, even at that impressive length, it was still too small to keep.

"It sucks that we had to throw my first catch back in," Nolan says out-of-the-blue, unknowingly echoing my thoughts as he casts his line out over the pristine lake surface.

I check my own line—no bites—and agree.

"Yeah, I know. But those are the rules, my friend. We have to abide by the water regulations for shit like that. Minnesota has strict guidelines for fish limits, possessions, and keeper sizes. It blows, but it's just the way it is."

Yeah, Nolan and I may be fishing on my own private lake, but I always follow the rules to the letter of the law.

Correct that—I always follow the rules *these days.*

There was a time not so long ago that I didn't follow rules at all.

Nope, I was Mr. Rule Breaker.

But then shit got a little out of hand, and the team hired Aubrey Shelburne, life coach extraordinaire, to whip my ass back into shape.

She did exactly that, and in the process we fell in love.

That's why I'm here today in the wilderness several miles outside Minneapolis. It's a beautiful June morning, and Aubrey and I are getting married in a couple of weeks. The ceremony will be held in a white-steeple church in the quaint little town right down the road.

Nolan's here to be my best man, which is perfect since Aubrey's sister, Lainey, is the matron of honor. She happens to be married to Nolan.

Speaking of our beautiful women... Aubrey and Lainey will be flying in to join us later this week—Saturday, to be exact.

Nolan and I came up to the lake house early to get in some quality bro time.

To kick things off, I asked him last night if he wanted to go fishing today. He claimed he was all in...until I told him what time we'd need to get up.

Man, I really thought he might bail.

"At dawn?" he exclaimed, looking none too happy.

We were kicking back outside on the upper deck off from my living room, watching the fireflies and drinking beer.

"You have got to be kidding me," he went on.

"Nope, sorry. I'm not. Early morning is when the fish are biting, my man."

"Shit, Brent. It's bad enough when we have to get up at ungodly hours for hockey practice. But this is the off-season and I'm enjoying sleeping in, thank you very much."

"Hey, I'm no early riser either," I replied, laughing. "But the fish don't care about our sleeping habits. We need to get our asses out on the lake early if we want to have any luck."

He sighed. "Hmm, I don't know if this country living is for me. But, what the hell, I'll give it a go."

I was surprised he relented so easily, as Nolan Solvenson really is a city guy at heart.

That's okay. He's taking to rural life just fine now.

But he sure wasn't this morning.

Despite having warned him that we'd be waking up extremely early, he was none too pleased when I sauntered into his bedroom at the ass crack of dawn.

It didn't help matters that, like a moose in heat, I bellowed, "Rise and shine, motherfucker. It's time to go reel us in some whoppers."

"Whopper this, Oliver," he grumbled, grabbing his junk.

In no way deterred by his belligerence, I volleyed back, "Fuck off, Solvenson."

Barefoot, I padded over to a big-ass window facing eastward, right in the line of the sun coming up over the horizon, and yanked on the shade.

Up it went, not only making one hell of a clatter, but also allowing the bright morning light to blast right in on Nolan.

Covering his eyes, he yelled, "What the hell? Do you have a death wish, Oliver?"

I just laughed. "Christ, you sure are one mean prick in the morning. I don't know how poor Lainey stands you."

"Pfft," he retorted, chuckling, "maybe she just knows the right way to wake me."

"Yeah, well…" I rolled my eyes. "I'm not doing *that*. And thanks, by the way. That is so not a visual of my soon-to-be sister-in-law that I care to have stuck in my head all day."

"Speak for yourself," he murmured. "*I* find it a rather inspiring visual."

"I bet you do. And just for that…" I popped up the shade of another window and was promptly met with more death threats.

"No, no, you don't want to kill me, Solvenson," I said.

Rolling onto his back, and covering his face with his forearm, he muttered, "Oh yeah? Why not?"

"First," I ticked off, "Aubrey would definitely seek revenge. And it wouldn't be your life that was in danger—it'd be your balls."

"Fuck." He lowered his hand to cover his nads. "Lainey wouldn't like that one bit."

"Exactly," I concurred. "That'd most definitely have the sisters fighting. And since I'd be dead, you'd have to deal with the two of them all on your own."

Nolan shuddered. "Jesus, say no more."

"So I get to live?"

"If it means I only have to deal with one Shelburne woman at a time, then yes, your life is no longer in danger."

"Phew." I blew out a faux relieved breath, complete with a dramatic forehead swipe.

The Shelburne sisters can be a handful sometimes, but you know what?

Neither Nolan, nor I, would have it any other way.

Aubrey is hot and sexy and keeps me on my toes. And from what Nolan tells me, Lainey does the same for him.

Nolan sat up in bed then and scrubbed his hand down the dark scruff on his face.

"So we're really going fishing today, eh?" he asked.

"You told me you wanted to try it," I reminded him. "And since there's a lake conveniently located right outside…"

"Okay," he relented. "Let's go do this."

So that's how we got to where we are right now—floating around in a canoe on the lake, lines cast out, waiting for another bite.

I'm actually glad Nolan didn't back out. This lake is brimming with walleye, trout, and bass. It'd be a shame to let a good fishing opportunity go to waste.

Before Aubrey, I never even thought to do constructive shit like this. The only thing I ever did on this lake was take girls out in the canoe so I could fuck them on the water.

Jesus, I'm glad those days are over.

It was fun for a while, sure, but in the end I was heading

nowhere fast.

This was all a couple of summers ago—pre-Aubrey, of course.

Nolan and my other linemate, Benny Perry, were up here at the lake house. All three of us were a bit of a mess back then, spending most of our time simply partying. We never went fishing that summer, not once. We were too busy getting drunk and screwing puck bunnies.

Glad that's all over now. The three of us have settled down and put our hard-partying ways behind us. Not only am I with Aubrey and Nolan with Lainey, but Benny, the biggest partier of us all, is himself in a serious relationship, with a woman named Eliza.

She has a cute baby, Ava, whom Benny adores. The fact that Ava is a child from another man has never deterred him from pursuing—and then committing to—her.

He's just a great guy like that.

I think that's why Coach Townsend, who happens to be Eliza's father, didn't murder my big lug of a teammate once their relationship came to light.

Good thing he didn't, seeing as Benny is an integral part of the team.

Big Benny will actually be joining us here at the lake house later tonight. Nolan and I couldn't leave him out of our no-women-allowed bro fest. Hell no!

I sigh as I think about the days ahead. This truly is our last hurrah before the wedding. Not that we have anything wild planned, since, like I said before, we're all real mellow now.

Then again, who knows?

When the three of us are left to our own devices, anything can happen.

Maybe we're not so mellow, after all.

After adjusting my line once more, I remark to Nolan, "It's good to be up here at the lake house once again, isn't it? Kind of like old times."

"It is," he agrees. "This place is pretty fucking awesome."

"You're not kidding, man."

For as much as I adore Las Vegas, where Aubrey and I make our home during the hockey season, I just fucking love Minnesota. It will always be my true home. My family still live here, and I grew up not too far from where we're at right now.

I guess that's why I was elated when Aubrey suggested we get married in this little town outside Minneapolis. She told me it felt right because we had met at the lake house, which is a whole other story unto itself.

I chuckle at *that* memory, and Nolan asks, "What's so funny, Brent?"

Still smiling, I reply, "I was just remembering how Aubrey and I first met."

Nolan, thinking it over for a sec, says, "It was at that end-of-summer party we had, right? That was our final blowout before training camp started that year.'"

"It was," I confirm. "And, yep, that's when Aubrey and I met. But, man, she and I sure hated each other at first."

"Dude, how could that be? She woke up in your bed the next morning."

I laugh. "Yeah, that's part of the reason *why* she hated me."

As Nolan fidgets with his line, he says, "Eh, it doesn't matter now. You two have come a long way since then."

I blow out a breath and have to agree, "Yeah, we sure have."

Nolan asks what time it is, so I grab my phone so I can check.

"Uh, looks like it's almost seven," I tell him, squinting to see the screen in the sunlight.

Nodding thoughtfully, he says, "That means it's about 5:00 out in Vegas."

"Hey, wait," I interject, "I just remembered Aubrey's bachelorette party was last night. Wonder if she, Lainey, and the girls are still out on the town."

Nolan chuffs, "No way, man. I don't know about the other girls, but we, my friend, have our women satisfied and tamed." He puffs out his chest, all masculine-like. "Guaranteed, Aubrey and Lainey had maybe one or two drinks, gossiped and giggled with their friends for an hour or so, and then wrapped up the party by midnight."

Jesting, I say, "So you don't think they're out partying in the wee hours of the night with a bunch of male strippers?"

We look at each other and burst out laughing.

"Yeah"—I nod—"no fucking way are they still out on the town."

"Nope," Nolan concurs. "In fact, scratch what I said earlier. I bet they were back home and in bed by eleven."

"Definitely."

While I imagine my beautiful Aubrey fast asleep in the big bed we share in our Las Vegas home, probably dreaming about our upcoming nuptials, Nolan calls out, "Hey, I think I got a bite."

TAKE IT OFF! TAKE IT *ALL* OFF!

AUBREY

"Ooh, baby, take it off! Take it *all* off!"

That's not me screaming to the hot, nearly naked man up on the stage.

Nope, it's Lainey, my wild and crazy younger sister.

Her long raven hair flies in my face as she starts doing her best heavy-metal head swing, chanting once more, "Take your clothes off, baby. Take...them...off."

Yep, it may be almost five in the morning out here in Sin City, but my bachelorette party is still going strong. Wonder what our men, Brent and Nolan, are doing in Minnesota right about now?

I bet they're sleeping.

Hell, that's what I'd be doing at this hour under normal circumstances. But my party is far from "normal circumstances." I knew we were in for a long night from the very beginning. Shit, we didn't even start the festivities till around midnight, kicking it off with a full-course dinner, followed by drinks at an after-hours club.

And here we are now—at a private strip club show that's been set up for me and my closest friends.

"Come onnnnn… Show us your junk," Lainey calls out to the stripper on the stage.

She wads up a fifty-dollar bill and tosses it up to him. I guess it's to sweeten the pot so he'll flash us.

Dancer guy picks up the money and un-crumples the bill to see what denomination it is.

Nodding approvingly, he drops the fifty into a nearby jar and shoots Lainey a wicked grin.

Uh-oh, it's on.

And it is.

The dancer sloooowly lowers his gold lamé shorts, just enough to give us an eyeful.

And what an eyeful we get.

"Holy shit, he's huge, Aubrey!" Lainey squeals, grabbing my arm.

"Hmm, he is rather well-endowed," I have to agree.

He dances and we ogle. And when he's finished, he exits stage right.

"Hmm, that was fun," I murmur.

"Indeed," Lainey says, nodding enthusiastically.

Since there's a short break before the next guy's set to begin, I turn to Lainey and say, "So, with all that whooping and hollering on your part, does that mean stripper dude's junk is bigger than Nolan's?"

"Hey now, hush your mouth," she admonishes. "I never said *that*, Aubrey."

Damn, despite her denial, I think I almost had her there.

Grrr...

It drives me nuts that Lainey's always bragging about the size of her husband's dick. I've been wondering for quite some time now just how much of that is bluster...and how much is fact.

Her husband is Nolan Solvenson, my fiancé Brent's best friend and linemate. I guess I could ask Brent, since I'm sure he's seen Nolan naked in the locker room, and probably the showers too.

But yeah, no, that might be too weird. Brent could think I want Nolan or something.

And let me assure you, I only have eyes for *my* man.

In any case, I suspect Nolan's cock is no larger than my soon-to-be husband's, seeing as Brent is plenty blessed in the peen department. Not to mention, based on what I just saw up on the stage, no way is stripper dude packing more meat than my guy.

But if he had been bigger than Nolan…well then, I finally would've known for certain that Brent wins for "biggest cock on the team."

When you think about it, though, if that's the case, then I'm the real winner.

Ah, too bad dear Lainey didn't slip up.

My sister catches me smirking and, misreading the situation, leans in and taunts, "Hmm, you're not fretting over the fact Brent is in no way bigger than Nolan, are you, Aubrey?"

"Pfft," I snort, "you wish."

She pats me on the shoulder, mock-comforting me.

Bitch!

"I don't have to wish, Aubs. I *know*. But don't be sad. I'm sure Brent's not *that* far behind in the ole big-cock department."

I push her away. "Shut up. And for the record, I'm not sad at all. Brag all you want. There's no way your man is bigger than mine."

With a spark of mischievousness igniting in her turquoise eyes, so like my own since we do in fact look a lot alike, she says, "I don't know if I believe you. I think we may need to have a dick measuring contest to end this speculation for good."

I nearly choke on my dirty martini.

Once I recover, I exclaim, "A dick measuring contest? Are you nuts?"

She frowns. "No, I don't think so."

"Like, you mean with the two of them together, Nolan and Brent?" I laugh. "They'd never go for that."

Lainey sure is a wild one. This is just ordinary conversation for her. That's why she's the perfect match for Nolan. Not only are they both sex-obsessed, but he's the only person on this planet who can keep her under control.

I guess he uses his super-sized cock to accomplish that feat.

Too bad he wasn't around earlier. He could've toned her down a notch before we all met up for my party.

But alas, he's up in Minnesota with Brent, doing Lord knows what and leaving me to deal with a totally unrestrained Lainey Shelburne.

"No, seriously, Aubrey," she continues, fixated on the contest idea. "I bet we could talk them into doing it."

See what I mean about unrestrained?

She's also unrelenting.

This girl is like a dog with a bone, no pun intended.

"Are you drunk?" I ask.

"No," she replies.

I sigh. "Just forget about it, Lainey. They'll never agree to it, okay?"

Unfazed, she continues, "Hey, you just gave me an idea with your silly accusation."

I wince. "Uh-oh. What kind of an idea are we talking about here?"

Lifting her martini glass and nodding to the contents, she says, "We just need to get our boys good and drunk. They'll agree to anything then. Plus, if they're really hammered, I bet they'll let us watch."

I snort, "You'd like that, wouldn't you? Seeing the boys whip out their junk, tape measures in hand."

She shrugs, and I roll my eyes so hard I'm surprised they don't fall back into my head.

This girl has cock on the brain.

"What?" she states indignantly. "Why are you rolling your eyes? Like you wouldn't enjoy *that* show too."

She kind of has a point, so I just shrug.

Lainey—dog with a bone, remember?—then says, "So back to the measuring contest… I'm thinking if it's a go then someone will need to observe. You know, to deter any cheating. And let's not forget that one of us will need to hold the tape and judge. So…" She raises her hand. "I volunteer."

See what I mean about cock-obsessed?

And wait a second here…

What did she just say?

"You're delusional." I scoff. "And let's be clear. You are *not* holding a tape measure anywhere near Brent's dick, you wicked bitch."

She laughs. "You think he's going to lose, don't you?"

I reach for her glass. "Okay, that's it. I'm cutting you off."

Swiftly moving her martini out of reach—guess she's not *that* drunk—she whines, "See, that's why you have to be there, Aubs. You can hold the tape for Brent, and I'll hold it for Nolan."

"Hold what for who?" Eliza, Benny Perry's girlfriend, chimes in.

She's just returned from the ladies' room. She was seated next to me before this crazy conversation got rolling. Lucky for her, she ran to the restroom with Chloe right before Lainey started up with her hair-brained dick-measuring idea.

Chloe is Dylan Culderway's wife. Dylan is a defenseman with the Wolves and a great friend to all the guys. He's not going up to Minnesota early to hang with them, though. Only because Chloe is pregnant.

It's so cute—Dylan is über-protective of his wife these days. There's no way he'd leave her all alone in Las Vegas.

Suddenly realizing that Eliza has returned from the restroom all by herself, and also in the interest of ending the dick-measuring contest craziness for good, I say, "Hey, Eliza, what happened to Chloe? Did you abandon her in the ladies' room?"

"No. She decided to take off." She snickers as she flips back her strawberry-blonde hair. "Chloe said she was *really* exhausted. I think she was just missing Dylan. It's probably not all that much fun not being able to drink with us."

I nod. "Yeah, I get that."

Of course, Lainey is listening in and interjects, "She can still watch men get naked and carry on with us. She's pregnant, ya know, not dead."

"Ignore her," I murmur to Eliza. "She's had *way* too many martinis."

Lainey smacks my arm. "I have not!"

It doesn't matter.

Since Eliza's had a few drinks of her own, she doesn't heed my advice, anyway.

Nope, she just leans right over me and says to Lainey, "Hey, between us, I think watching the strippers worked Chloe up. Dylan is around, you know, and I bet she just wanted to go home so she could jump him. Speaking of which, that's exactly what I need to do with Benny when *I* get home. His flight to Minneapolis doesn't leave till later today, so there's plenty of time."

"Lucky for you." Lainey purses her lips into a full pout. "Looks like everyone will be getting dick except for me. Damn it, I hate that Nolan is away."

"I won't be getting any," I remind her. "Brent's gone too, you know?"

Lainey nods as she concedes, "That's true."

Smirking, Eliza smugly retorts, "Ah, too bad for the both of you."

Hmm, I can't let that go.

I volley back, "No worries, Eliza. I have Brent 51 at home. He's in my nightstand and can take care of the job for now."

Lainey snickers knowingly, but Eliza's brow furrows.

"What's a Brent 51?" she asks.

"It's a sex toy that's really called Area 51," Lainey informs her all too excitedly. "I have one too, which I will *definitely* be putting to use later today."

Whoa, Eliza's interest is piqued. Her big green eyes are wide and inquisitive. And that's when the horror hits me—I never got around to giving her an Area 51 sex toy back when I was making sure all the hockey wives and girlfriends had one.

Good God, no!

"Girl." I place my hand on her arm. "You do not know what you're missing. But never fear. We can remedy that."

"Mmm-hmmm," Lainey murmurs, nodding profusely.

My sister seems calmer now that she knows she'll be getting some later, even if it is with a glowing, bright green plastic penis.

It wiggles *and* warms, though, as you heat up.

So there is that.

With a promise to Eliza that I'll get her an Area 51 toy soon, I say, "Then you can have some real fun too."

"Sounds good, Aubrey," she replies. "I'll need it once Benny's away. Thanks."

I assure her that she'll *really* be thankful once she tries out her new toy.

We talk and laugh about that until the next stripper comes out.

And then…*whoa!*

New stripper dude looks a lot like Brent—dark hair, deep brown eyes, strong jaw, totally buff bod, and a really big bulge in the pants he's about to tear off.

And there they go…

Sigh.

Yeah, Brent 51 is definitely getting a workout tonight.

WHAT'S GOOD FOR THE GOOSE...

BRENT

Nolan hooks a nice big perch and we cook it up for dinner at night, along with loaded baked potatoes, a spring green salad, and some fresh asparagus.

We save a bunch of food for Benny since he'll be coming in soon and will most likely be hungry as hell.

Let me tell you, that guy eats a lot.

Benny also has a major penchant for donuts, but there are no sweets in the house.

I'm sure he'll remedy that soon enough. Wait till he sees there's a bakery in town.

Turns out, as we discover a short while later, Benny's far more than merely hungry—he's "fucking famished."

Those are his exact words as he walks through the front door, his long-again dark blond hair flowing down to his shoulders.

The dude could totally pass for Thor. Everyone tells him that, especially since he's as big and built as the guy in the movies.

Striding off in the direction of the kitchen, sloughing off bags as he goes, Benny says, "What's for dinner, anyway? Whatever it is, it smells fucking delicious."

"Nolan caught a fish this morning," I tell him when I catch up. "We fried it up for dinner tonight."

He stops and turns to Nolan, who's following closely behind.

With pure I'm-about-to-fuck-with-you flickering in his green eyes, Benny says, "No fucking way. What kind of fish did you catch, Nolan? A minnow?"

"Ha-fucking-ha," Nolan chuffs. "It was big enough to cook for dinner, I can tell you that. But now that you mention it, Perry, the piece we saved for you is only about minnow-sized."

"You hear that, big guy," I chime in. *Ah, fucking with this guy is just too much fun.* "That means it's about the size of your cock."

Benny snorts, "Fuck you both."

Nolan volleys back, "What, with your minnow-sized dick? No, thanks. I think I'll pass."

We all lose it then.

Shit, man, it's good having these guys back here with me. It's kind of like old times, but less blurry.

About fifteen minutes in, as Benny is devouring his heated-up meal, I remark, "Jesus, don't they feed people on commercial flights these days? I'm glad Nolan and I chartered a private jet."

"Must be nice," Benny mumbles around another ravenous bite. "But seriously, even in first class the portions are miniscule."

"Again, like your dick," Nolan interjects with a smartass chuckle.

I swear razzing each other over the size of our junk never gets old.

Never, man, never.

Benny shoots Nolan the one-finger salute and says to us both, "It's not just the mini-bites they serve you on the plane that has me starving. Eliza fucking wore me out before I left Las Vegas."

Nolan raises a brow. "Is that so?"

"Uh-huh," Benny mumbles around another mouthful of food.

He finishes and pushes his plate to the side.

And then he explains…

"So, get this. Eliza comes in at like, I don't know, maybe six or seven in the morning. And the girl freaking attacks me. I mean, dude, I wake up and she's riding my fucking cock like I'm a horse and she's in the Kentucky Derby." He smirks. "Not that I'm complaining or anything. I'll be her Justify anytime."

I hear only one thing in Benny's sordid little tale, and it has me bellowing, "Six or seven in the morning? What the actual fuck?"

"Yep," Benny confirms. "That's what time Eliza came in. An Uber dropped her off. And from what she told me later, after we'd had our fun, the party had ended only ten minutes prior to that."

"What the hell?" I growl. "What kind of crap were they getting up to at Aubrey's bachelorette party? I thought it was supposed to be a chill event?"

Looking none too happy himself, Nolan murmurs tightly, "Clearly, it was not if they stayed out all night."

"So much for 'in bed by eleven,'" I snort. "So much for having our girls tamed."

I was crazy to ever entertain such an idea. The Shelburne women are wild at heart. There's no "taming" them.

Benny fills us in on how the party supposedly started late. "According to Eliza, they didn't even eat dinner till around midnight. Then they went out for a bunch of drinks and later hit up some private male revue."

Nolan doesn't like that one bit.

"Strippers, eh?" he chuffs. "And Lainey used to bitch at me for going to female strip clubs."

He shakes his head, but before he gets all up on his high horse, I remind him, "That was only because you often *slept* with the dancers, remember?"

Sheepishly, he remarks, "Oh yeah, that's right."

When Benny and I start smirking, he says, "Hey, no giving

me attitude. That crap happened long before I was involved with Lainey."

"As I recall," Benny counters, "you two were on a break when you last visited a club."

"Okay, okay. So I was a real prick in the past," Nolan replies. "But I'm fucking devoted to Lainey now. Not to mention, I don't have to *like* the thought of her watching strange men take off their clothes."

Benny nods thoughtfully. "Hmm, I see what you're saying. But I don't really mind if Eliza watches dudes get naked. Of course, I got to reap the rewards. And let me tell you, based on how horny my girl was it must've been one hell of a show."

"Okay, okay." I hold up my hand, not wanting to hear another word since *my* woman didn't have me around to get off on. "Enough already."

I make a silent vow to myself that when Aubrey gets here I am going to fuck her so hard that all memories of those dudes fly straight out of her head.

From the tight set of Nolan's jaw, I suspect he's thinking the same thing about Lainey.

Damn, Benny's lucky he already had the chance to take care of business with Eliza.

One thing the boys lay out then, which I'm in total agreement on now, is that I get to have a bachelor party *with* strippers.

We'll have to hurry, though, in order to get it in before

Saturday since that's when the girls are due in.

"We'll just set it up for the night before," Nolan says when I raise this concern. "We'll have the strippers come to the house to keep things on the down-low. We don't need the town's residents ratting us out. And let me tell you, boys, this is not going to be G-rated entertainment."

"Fucking A," Benny chimes in.

"That's right," I concur. "You bet your ass it's not."

Hey, what can I say?

What's good for the goose is good for the gander.

THE BOYS WILL FREAKING LOVE THIS

AUBREY

There's really nothing left for me to do in Las Vegas in terms of wedding prep, and with my bachelorette party over and in the books, I decide to talk to Lainey and Eliza about heading up to the lake house early.

"Let's totally surprise the boys," I say once we're all convened, albeit only electronically.

We're on a three-way Skype call, and I can't help but smile when Lainey and Eliza blurt out in unison, "Yes!"

Eliza goes on to say, "I love that idea, Aubrey. My parents are planning to watch Ava while I'm away, anyway. Well, until they come up right before the wedding, that is. Drew gets her then.

But enough about that." She sighs. "Bottom line is my mom and dad would love to have Ava in their care earlier than planned."

"Awesome," I reply. "Then we're all in agreement?"

I'm met with murmurs of assent.

"Okay, let me log onto my laptop and see if I can change our flights from, say, Saturday to Friday?"

"Sounds good," Lainey says.

Grabbing my laptop off a nearby table, I pull up our reservations.

After scrolling through several available options, I tell the girls, "Okay, it looks like we can definitely fly into Minneapolis on Friday. That means we could roll into the lake house by about ten that night. How's that sound?"

"Works for me," Lainey says.

"Yeah, me too," Eliza agrees.

With the girls on board, I change the reservations and receive confirmation.

"Ladies," I announce, "we are all set."

Lainey squeals, "This is going to be so much fun. Surprising the guys, I can't wait!"

I add, "They're going to be so shocked. I bet they'll freaking love that we came in early."

Eliza, though she likes our plan, laments, "I just wish Dylan and Chloe could join us."

Chloe has really become a part of our girl crew. But there's no way she'd fly up early with us. Not only is Dylan not even at the lake house, but with a baby on the way they're both in full nesting mode.

Oh, well, that's okay. We'll see them soon enough at the wedding. They promised they wouldn't miss Brent and me tying the knot for the world.

I remind the girls that we may have a chance to do something like this again, where Chloe can accompany us.

"After all," I add slyly, "Eliza's not married to Benny...*yet*."

Lainey chimes in, "Yes, Eliza, when is that big lug of a man going to make an honest woman out of you?"

Eliza rolls her emerald eyes. She is so not a traditionalist.

"Who knows," she replies. "But it doesn't matter. I'm happy with the way things are right now."

See what I mean?

"Still," the ever-persistent Lainey presses, "I bet when you're ready, you could totally bribe him with donuts to buy you the biggest diamond ring on the planet."

Everyone knows about Benny's penchant for donuts, so I jump right in on that too.

"She's right," I say. "Donuts are like crack to that man. They're his kryptonite."

Eliza snorts. "No way. You're both wrong. Sex is Benny's kryptonite."

"Ooh, use that then," Lainey says.

I roll my eyes. "Any chance to insert sex, Lain, and you just can't resist."

"Ha, ha. You just said 'insert' and 'sex.'"

I glare at my sister. "Some of the shit you find amusing, Lainey... I swear you're like a female version of Beavis and Butthead."

Lainey snaps, "Hey, I can only be one or the other. They happen to be two separate characters, Aubrey."

"You would know," I mutter.

"Would you two just stop," Eliza groans, even though she's laughing right along with us. "And for the record, I'm not 'using' anything to make Benny marry me. When he's ready, he'll ask."

She's so damn chill. I wish I could be more like her. I need to remember that not everything has to happen at once. Things have a way of working themselves out over time.

Although a little nudge can never hurt, right? If sex is Benny's kryptonite, then why not add something to Eliza's arsenal?

I make a mental note to pack that Area 51 sex toy I promised her.

Come to think of it, I should really pack two. Who knows who else up at the lake house might need one?

Hmm, guess I am as much of a perv as my sister.

Oh well...

With that decided, I say to Eliza, "Hey, I'll bring along that gift I promised you."

Lainey snickers knowingly, but Eliza seems perplexed.

"Huh? What gift?"

"Buzzzz, buzz, buzz," Lainey says. "Ring a bell?"

Eliza gets it then. "Oh, you're talking about that sex toy you told me about at the club."

"Ha," I scoff, "you sound so unimpressed. I promise you, woman, this is not your everyday, average sex toy."

Lainey chimes in, "Yeah, you'll see. Just one word of advice— maybe close the blinds before you turn it on."

I laugh, and Eliza asks, "Do I even want to know what that means?"

"Nope," Lainey and I blurt out together.

I then add, "You'll find out soon enough."

"You two." Eliza laughs. "You're both so off the hook."

I assure her then, "Just wait till we get to Minnesota. You're about to see off the hook."

5

I'M NOT SURPRISED, YOU'RE SURPRISED

BRENT

My bachelor party is in full swing.

Well, I should clarify. It's not really a *party* party. It's more like five women dancing around seductively in nothing but G-strings for me and the boys.

The music beats out in the background, the reverberating bass punctuating the strippers' sexy moves.

We're in my upstairs living room, and the floor-to-ceiling windows serve to reflect back to us the seductive scene.

Yeah, the drapes are wide open.

But it's nighttime, so who cares?

There's nothing but wilderness out there, anyway. And call

me crazy, but I don't think the owls give a shit about tits and asses.

Damn, but I sure do.

I hate to say it, but these girls have my full attention, particularly when the tall, blonde dancer starts rubbing her double Ds against the little redhead's full Bs.

There's just something so fucking hot about the whole tawdry scene.

Maybe it's the realistic expressions of lust on their faces, or that they can't stop gasping every time their hardened nipples touch.

Whatever it is, I think they're truly enjoying this shit.

Fuck.

Aubrey would kill me right now if she saw me, especially since my traitorous dick is stirring in my pants.

Good thing she doesn't come in till tomorrow. That gives me time to take a bunch of cold showers and whack off like crazy till she gets here.

Once she does arrive, though, I am going to have her in so many fucking ways…

Just then the boob-rubbing girls move closer to me. Like we're talking directly in front of the plushy chair I'm slouched down in.

I scoot back an inch.

Yeah, best to avoid too much temptation.

I haven't touched a single girl tonight—I've just merely watched them—but I still feel a little guilty and a whole lot dirty.

I remind myself that this is no worse than watching porn. It's probably tamer, actually. It just happens to be live and not on a screen.

I look over at Nolan and Benny, who are seated at opposite ends of the sofa. They seem to be enjoying themselves too.

And no wonder.

The other three strippers have migrated to in front of them, where they're doing, uh, all sorts of interesting things.

Wait, is that girl licking the other girl's pussy?

No, no, she has on a G-string. They both do, thank God.

I'd feel even worse about this than I already do if they were totally nude.

Shit.

I sigh.

I already feel kind of bad, and now I'm kind of ready for this show to end. It's hot, sure, but I love Aubrey far too much to *really* get into it.

Call me whipped or whatever, I just don't care.

I have a feeling Nolan and Benny feel the same way. I'm sure they're enjoying the show, as well—they are men, after all—but they don't look like they're over-the-top into it.

Glancing down at my phone on the side table, I check to see what time it is.

Hmm, it's after ten so there's only about fifteen minutes left before the strippers are supposed to pack up and leave. Good.

I relax, content in knowing that this will be over soon.

But then the stripper with the double Ds stops what she's doing and asks me, "Are you the one getting hitched, honey?"

"Um, yeah," I carefully reply.

"Oh, fabulous," she squeals. "That means you, good-looking, get the special *special* show."

"And what exactly does that entail?" I query, brow furrowing.

"This."

She crawls up onto the arms of the chair, placing her knees on one side and her hands on the other.

Her body is basically stretched out over me as she asks, "Are you ready for the next part, big boy?"

"I, uh…"

Crap, her massive boobs are almost touching my lap.

That is so not good.

Before I can put a stop to this nonsense, and before I do something really stupid that I'll regret forever, the redhead hands me a paddle.

"Go ahead and spank her," she says nonchalantly. "By the way, she likes it extra hard."

Oh fuck.

"Wait." I try to hand the paddle back. "I don't think I want to do that."

"Sure you do," the redhead insists.

Thankfully, Nolan notices what's going on and comes over to put a stop to this now off-the-rails show.

But he gets no further than, "Hey, I think we're done—" before he's handed a paddle of his own.

"You get to go next, handsome," the redhead says. "Or you can both spank her at the same time if you'd like. She'd *really* enjoy that."

Help?

Benny is still over on the sofa, his jaw dropping when he hears that part.

Shit, this must look like a kinky setup for a porno.

I mean, let's see…We have the obligatory naked blonde with her ass up in the air, looking like she's crawling across my chair, and me, paddle in hand, appearing as if I'm about to spank her.

Oh, and let's not forget the naked redhead and paddle-wielding Nolan.

Jesus.

Just then, when I can't imagine things getting any worse, they do.

Yep, that's right—I hear the one voice I would never want to hear while in a position like this.

But hear her I do.

"Brent?"

"Aubrey?" I squeak.

Fuck, this is really, really bad timing for my soon-to-be wife to show up.

What's she doing here anyway? It's not Saturday.

Aubrey repeats my name, sounding angrier than ever when she goes on to say, "Is that you under that…that…*woman*? Answer me, damn it!"

"Um, uh…" is about all I can muster at the moment.

I am so busted.

Nolan, sensing the catastrophe at hand, reaches out, and with one arm, lifts the stripper off of me.

Thank you, thank you.

I guess he realizes then that Aubrey is not alone, since he starts biting out a litany of "Oh fuck."

Fuck is right.

Here comes fiery Lainey, heading right over to us.

She's on a mission too, stomping her way toward Nolan.

He blubbers, "Ah, honey, I can ex—"

But she walks right past him, cutting him off with one mean-ass glare.

We then watch in horror—and, oh hell, maybe some amusement too—as Laincy grabs hold of Double Ds long blonde hair, hauls her ass back, and starts wailing on her.

That's pretty much when *all* hell breaks loose.

6

LITTLE HELLCATS

AUBREY

My little sister, she always has my back.

And I have hers.

That's why, when the blonde stripper chick with the giant boobs gets the upper hand, I race over to the rescue.

Nolan is doing his part to try and separate my sister from the dancer, but I get the job done when I yank the bitch off Lainey.

"Get the hell off of her!" I scream in Blondie's face.

And then I wind up, ready to sock her one.

But before my punch can land, someone grabs my fist.

Huh?

"What the hell?"

I spin around, and it's Brent.

I hiss, "You, you… You cheating bastard!"

I'm still mad at him, so I decide to hit him instead of the stripper.

But first, I grind out, "You're an asshole. And to think I came up early for *this*."

I try to smack him then, but he's much faster than me. Easily, he catches my hand.

Damn hockey reflexes!

Spinning me around, he wraps me up in his strong arms.

He ends up behind me, holding me securely as I start to struggle. I might normally like this position, but not with what I just witnessed.

"Let me go," I spit out.

"Stop fighting me, Aubrey," he hisses in my ear. "I can explain everything."

"Explain?" I pant, going lax.

Yeesh, kicking ass is exhausting.

Once I catch my breath, I seethe, "I saw you with my own two eyes, you jerk. That girl was practically in your lap, and you were about to smack her ass with a paddle."

I look around, an idea brewing.

"Where is that paddle, anyway?" I mutter.

I see it, but Lainey's beaten me to it. And she's using the paddle in the way I was hoping to if I could've escaped Brent.

Yep, Lainey is whacking the hell out of the blonde *and* the redhead.

It's funny, actually.

Both strippers are running around, jumping in the air, yelping and yapping as they try to avoid my sister's angry swats.

If I weren't so infuriated, I'd be laughing my ass off. But as it is, I just look around to see what else is going on.

The other three strippers have thrown on their shirts and are watching safely from the sidelines, way over on the other side of the living room.

Guess in the stripper world, everyone's out for themselves.

I scan around for Nolan.

Oh, there he is, chilling not far from us.

"What are you doing just standing there?" I snap at him.

Brent's arms tighten around me. He knows I have a love-hate relationship with Nolan, which is leaning heavily towards hate right about now.

"Go help my sister," I hiss.

"Why would I do that? I'm enjoying the show far too much," he snipes back, smirking. "Besides, Lainey seems to be doing fine all on her own."

"Ugh, you, you…"

He makes me so mad that I start struggling again. If I can just get away from Brent, I can smack Nolan upside his smug head so hard that his teeth will jingle.

He sees me trying to break free and steps well out of hitting range. Smart move.

"Jesus," he mutters, "you Shelburne women sure are violent."

Giving up, since escaping Brent's solid grasp is again a lost cause, I retort, "Like you don't secretly love it."

Cocking his head, Nolan says, "You know what? I kind of do, actually."

Disgusted, I scoff, "You're twisted, Solvenson."

"So says the woman who came out of the corner swinging."

Brent, who's been fairly quiet up to this point, probably to avoid my wrath, says wearily, "Would you two just stop."

Suddenly realizing I haven't seen Eliza or Benny since this melee began, I ask Brent what happened to them.

"Where did they go?"

He shrugs, which feels kind of good since I'm pressed up so close to him. "I don't know, Aubrey."

Just as I'm allowing myself to enjoy the feel of a deliciously firm Brent Oliver, I remember something—I'm supposed to be mad at this man!

Snapping to my senses, I warn, "I expect a full explanation, buddy. I want to hear about everything that happened here tonight. And you better not have cheated on me or the wedding is off."

"I didn't cheat, Aubrey," he assures me softly.

And you know what?

I believe him.

But I'm still pissed in general. Anger doesn't dissipate that quickly.

I search again for Nolan, as he's usually a good target for my ire. But he's on the other side of the room now, busy refereeing the Lainey vs. Blonde and Redhead fight.

"It's about time," I mutter.

He's trying—in vain, I might add—to separate my fiery sister from the two strippers. Lainey has them in headlocks on either side of her.

I can't help but snicker. She really is a badass.

Nolan finally succeeds in breaking everyone apart. And once the strippers are released, they scamper away.

My sister, looking up at Nolan, just kind of collapses into him. She's clearly exhausted as he holds onto her sweetly.

Okay, okay.

Nolan may annoy the fuck out of me most days, but I have to admit he really is Lainey's rock.

He disengages from her long enough to pay the strippers and send them on their way.

As they're heading down the stairs, counting their cash, I notice that they don't seem fazed at all by what just happened. I suppose stripping for private parties is often dangerous work. Tonight is probably just another ordinary day on the job.

Yeesh.

Once the strippers are gone, Brent finally loosens his hold on me.

"Are you going to be good?" he asks before he completely lets go.

I shrug him off and spin around.

Then I stick my tongue out at him.

Rolling his gorgeous whiskey eyes at me, he says, "That's real mature, Aubrey. Maybe *you* need a paddling."

Like he's been struck with an idea, he cocks a brow.

Brat.

He's employing a move he knows drives me nuts.

Of course, it works. I can't help it. My lady bits come to life.

Yes, please.

Ugh, I need to refocus on Lainey and Nolan.

Er, well maybe not, seeing as they're totally sucking face now.

"God, could his tongue get any farther down her throat," I mutter.

Brent just laughs.

Since my sister and Nolan look like they might start screwing in the middle of the living room, I turn away.

That means the only thing left for me to focus on is Brent.

"Forgive me?" he rasps when our eyes meet.

I want an explanation even though I know in my heart he did nothing wrong.

Hell, who am I to cast aspersions?

I did my own fair share of ogling at naked bodies at my own stripper party just a few nights ago.

So, tentatively, I say, "I guess."

"Ah, Aubrey…" Brent takes me in his arms again, but this time it's to kiss me.

I let him, and we start making out like crazy…until Nolan interrupts us.

"Hey," he yells over. Lainey is still in his arms, nuzzling his neck. "Where in the hell are Benny and Eliza?"

Brent, leaning back, replies, "I don't know, man. We noticed they were missing, but I have no idea where they wandered off to."

Just then, from down the hall where the bedrooms are located, cries of, "Oh, Benny. Yes, yes, yes, right there. Harder, big boy, harder," ring out.

"All righty then," I say. "I think we just found them."

I turn to say something to my sister, but she's already heading off arm in arm with Nolan.

"Wonder where they're going?" I remark sarcastically to Brent.

"Off to Nolan's bedroom to do what Benny and Eliza are clearly doing?" he replies.

"Yep," I sigh. "It would seem so. So what do we do now?"

Brent raises a brow, a clear invitation.

"What do you think we should do, Aubrey?" he purrs. "Maybe

head down to our own bedroom and have some fun too?"

Oh my God, I should say no. But I have no resistance when it comes to this man.

"Hmm, maybe," I murmur. Then, smiling slyly, I add, "There is one condition, though, Brent."

"And what would that be, Aubrey?" he asks.

"Bring the paddle."

PADDLE PLAY

BRENT

Kissing my way up Aubrey's silky soft legs, I promise her, "I am going to make you feel so good, baby. You'll know then that I love you and only you."

It's true. I am going to prove to her that she's the only woman who matters to me. Fuck those strippers, landing me in hot water like this. Thank God Aubrey's letting me make it up to her.

I have to admit, though, that it's because of the strippers that there's so much sexual energy coursing through this house tonight. I feel it now; it's in the air and in my whole body.

That's probably why I tore off Aubrey's clothes the second we closed our bedroom door.

She must've felt it too, because she made just as short of work out of my apparel.

I'm glad the energy's not waning. It's still powerful, so much so that Aubrey's freaking trembling.

Though that may be because my mouth is on her pussy, my lips brushing over her folds, my tongue working her swollen clit.

When I pull back to take a breath, she begs, "Brent, don't stop. Don't tease me like that."

"Ah," I counter, chuckling, "but it's so much fun to keep you waiting, sweetheart. I love when you ache for me."

"I do, Brent, "she sighs. "I'll always ache for you."

She arches her back, inviting me to get back to what I was doing.

Oh hell, I can't resist. I give her a touch of my tongue, savoring her sweetness.

A few seconds later, when I have her right where I want her, I fucking devour her.

Aubrey loves it. She starts grinding into me, panting and mewling like a kitten.

Damn, I like her undone like this. I like feeling her lose control.

Besides playing really fucking good hockey, this is something I do *extremely* well.

"Come for me, baby," I murmur against her soft folds, nudging with my nose where I know she wants my tongue again.

"Then stop talking," she cries out, "and make it happen, Brent."

"Demanding little thing," I tease.

She's so close, but I need something from her first...

"I'll put my tongue right here..." I give her a light brush with the tip. "...if you tell me you've forgiven me."

"Yes," she pants. "I know you didn't touch any of them. I know nothing happened."

"It didn't, baby, I swear. I love you far too much to jeopardize us."

"Brent, I know that. So, unh, pleaseeee..."

I can't torture her a second longer. I finally give her what she wants, and seconds later, she is coming so hard against my mouth that I almost lose it myself.

But not yet...

Kissing my way up her stomach and over her luscious full breasts, I settle my body between her legs.

"I want you so much right now, baby," I groan.

"So take me, Brent."

That's all I need to hear. I thrust into her, and together we pant and sweat and fuck like animals.

It's unbridled and raw, but that's okay. I'll make love to her later. We need this roughness right now.

Aubrey grabs my ass with one hand and yanks my hair with the other.

I grasp her butt cheeks and fuck her hard.

But then I have another idea…

Snatching up the paddle that I brought along like she asked me to, I pull out, flip her over onto her stomach, and smack her once with the flat wooden base.

"Brent," Aubrey yelps, surprised.

Oh shit.

"Is it too much?" I check.

"No, no, not at all." She relaxes. "Try it again. I actually kind of like it."

"Ah, that's my girl."

I give her ass another whack with the paddle…then I caress the small pink spot.

"You're such a bad girl, Aubrey," I rasp. "Showing up early and unannounced, jumping on the strippers—"

"Yes, Brent, I am bad," she says, squirming beneath me. "You should definitely punish me some more."

Shit, she does fucking love this.

I do too.

I'm so fucking hard right now that my dick is about to explode, especially when she pushes her ass up in the air and begs me for more.

I give her another whack, and she moans in pleasure.

Fuck, I can't take this much longer. I need to be back inside her.

I rub my cock over the red spots I've left on her bottom, and then I spread her wide.

"You ready for me?" I ask.

"Always, Brent, always…"

"Ahh, yes…" I slide back into her.

Wow, I thought she was wet before. That was fucking nothing.

I reach around to toy with her clit and start fucking her again. She shatters, her pussy convulsing so hard around my cock that I end up coming right along with her.

Hmm, I think the paddle's definitely going back to Vegas with us.

8

KEEPING THE BOYS IN LINE

AUBREY

All is forgiven with our guys.

Well, I think it is. I know I've fully forgiven Brent.

For the rest of the crew, I'm basing that on the fact that everyone ended up in bed with their respective partners last night.

Now that it's the next morning, we're all at breakfast. And no one has yet mentioned the stripper fiasco. Yeah, I'm pretty sure we've all moved on.

I look around. Everyone seems so happy. And they sure are loving their food.

That's reassuring since Brent and I dragged our butts out

of bed extra early so we could make homemade pancakes for everyone. We had a chance to talk about things we'd not discussed last night as we prepped ingredients. I explained how I only wanted to surprise him by flying in a day early.

"Well, you sure did that," he said, chuckling as he whipped the batter. "Nolan and Benny seemed just as shocked to see Lainey and Eliza as I was to see you. Not to mention, those strippers had no idea what they were in for."

"Yes, about those strippers…" I raised a brow, flipping my raven locks angrily over my shoulder. "Was that Nolan and Benny's idea? Or was it yours?"

"Does it matter?" he asked. "I thought we worked this out last night in bed."

He waggled his brows, and I laughed.

"We did," I acquiesced.

And then, because it doesn't really matter anymore, I let it go.

So here we are, seated around the big farmhouse table in the dining room, enjoying a second helping of flapjacks.

I look around at everyone once more, smiling at this great group of people I have the honor of calling my friends.

Some of their antics make me laugh outright, like now…

Nolan and Lainey are freaking feeding each other—God help us—and Benny and Eliza are discussing what else but donuts.

I listen to that discussion since I'd rather hear about bakery goods than watch the nauseating display of affection between

Lainey and Nolan.

There Nolan goes, licking syrup off Lainey's chin.

Ugh.

Before I gag, or regurgitate my own pancakes—which I ate without assistance from Brent, by the way—I turn my full attention to Eliza and Benny.

"Yes, I'm sure there's a store in town that sells those chocolate-frosted donuts you like so much." I hear Eliza say to Benny.

"I sure hope so," he replies dejectedly. "Otherwise, I'm fucked."

"Jeez, Benny, donuts aren't *that* important."

He gasps at Eliza's offensive-to-him words. "I'll try and forget you said that, woman."

Snickering, I nudge Brent. "Your teammate really is obsessed with donuts," I whisper.

"Ha, you don't know the half of it," Brent quietly replies. "Coach caught him with half a dozen Krispy Kremes right before one of the playoff games and almost benched him for the night."

"No way," I gasp. "How'd Benny talk his way out of that one?"

"He didn't. Eliza saved his ass."

"Hmm, lucky for Benny he dates the coach's daughter, right?"

"Right."

Lainey takes a break from Nolan's mouth—yes, I looked over and they've progressed to kissing—long enough to ask, "What are you two whispering about over there, Aubrey?"

I shrug and reply, "Oh, nothing."

Then I remember I have an errand to run today, so I ask, "Hey, are you still coming with me into town this afternoon to pick up my gown?"

Ahh, my wedding dress...

It's a beautiful couture creation—a strapless, flowy piece of art adorned with intricate lace and pearl beadwork. The girls packed their bridesmaid dresses after our final fittings in Las Vegas, but mine was too bulky. I made arrangements instead to have it shipped to a bridal shop here in town.

"It's coming in today?" Lainey asks.

"Yes, it's supposed to be at the store by noon."

Eliza jumps in, "Ooh, can I come with?"

"Of course," I reply, smiling. "I want all my best girls with me."

Brent glances over at Nolan and Benny, and says with a sly smirk, "Looks like we're on our own again today, boys."

Benny just nods, but Nolan, always up for urging crap on, says, "Cool. Wonder what kind of trouble we can get into this time."

He's joking, but Lainey nonetheless smacks him on the arm.

"Heyyy," he protests.

"Hey this," she retorts. "There had better not be any more trouble with you, mister. I haven't fully forgotten about last night's antics."

Guess not all is completely forgiven. Or maybe my sister is just getting Nolan back in line. When I really think about it, I have to say that they keep each other in check. Whatever they have works.

Quietly, Nolan murmurs, "Okay, hon. I was just kidding."

Lainey seems satisfied with his response, but I'm not so sure *I* believe him.

Turning to Brent, I narrow my eyes. "Promise me you'll all behave today."

He raises a brow. "Behave? We're not dogs, Aubrey."

"Ha." I laugh. "After what I witnessed last night, I'm not so sure about that."

"Okay, okay," he concedes sheepishly. "I deserve that. But I swear to you, despite Nolan's ramblings"—he rolls his eyes over at his friend, who just shrugs all innocent-like—"there'll be no more bad behavior."

I believe Brent.

But to play it on the safe side, I encourage Lainey and Eliza to make their men swear to behave as well.

An hour later, all of us are feeling great as we head off to pick up my dress.

Hmm, I just hope everything keeps going this smoothly.

9

TROUBLE ALWAYS FINDS US

BRENT

I made a promise to Aubrey, and I intend to keep it.

That's why, when Nolan and Benny ask me what we should do today while the women are at the dress shop, I come up with the only surefire thing I know will keep us out of trouble.

"Let's get in a good hard skate."

We're still seated at the dining room table, but the dishes have been cleared and the ladies are gone.

Now it's just coffee and the guys.

Benny takes a sip from his cup of steaming brew and says, "Uh, dude, I know you're not thinking straight with the big day coming up and all, but you do realize that it's fucking summer out there, right?"

I retort, "I'm not talking about skating outdoors, ass. We can skate at my folks' place."

Benny sheepishly replies, "Oops, I forgot there's a rink at your parents' house. I guess when I think of Minnesota, my mind just immediately goes to skating out on some frozen pond somewhere."

Hmm, it does make sense, in a weird Benny kind of way.

Shaking my head, I continue, "Okay, so we can skate over there. The rink is in great shape still, and there's tons of hockey equipment just lying around from me and my dad. We should be set."

"That's right," Nolan chimes in. "I almost forgot that your father played professional hockey too."

Benny snorts, "How could you have forgotten that? Billy Oliver is the legacy Golden Boy here is always striving to live up to."

I shoot Benny the one-finger salute, but the truth is he's right. My dad won two Stanley Cups back in his day. And I'm still stuck at one.

Ugh.

I hope to change that stat this upcoming season. Good thing I have a feeling it's going to be our best yet.

It better be, damn it! I want another Stanley Cup!

"Okay," I say on a sigh, getting back on task. "Enough about my dad. Do you guys want to skate or not?"

"Sure, I'm in," Nolan replies.

"Me too," Benny concurs.

"Okay, then." I stand up. "Let's do this."

An hour later, the three of us are at my parents' place. Behind their big house—I guess you could call it a mansion—stands the building that houses the indoor rink.

It really is state-of-the-art in every way, which makes the guys let out low whistles when we walk inside.

"Damn, Oliver, you had it made growing up," Nolan marvels.

Benny shakes his head. "You're not fucking kidding, dude. I can't even…"

Yeah, it was pretty cool being the son of a hockey god.

Still is, really.

But it's even better when I can share the perks with my best friends, like I'm doing today.

After we gear up in the locker room, we head out onto the ice.

"Fuck, this is great, isn't it?" I call out to my teammates, who are trailing behind since my ass is moving. "I fucking love the ice, man."

Nolan catches up to me and, turning to skate backward, agrees, "It does feel good. Even though it's only been a couple of weeks since we were practicing every damn day."

Benny glides to us in time to hear that last bit.

"Ugh," he groans. "Let's not talk about those dreadful playoffs."

I sigh. This year's postseason wasn't good. We lost in the second round.

But because I'm the captain and it's up to me to keep morale up, I assure the guys, "Hey, we'll do better next season."

"We better," Nolan grumbles.

"For sure," Benny echoes.

We're all fierce competitors. That's why I know in my heart that the Wolves will make a strong comeback.

Suddenly feeling really fucking pumped, I start skating fast as hell, leaving the guys behind. They call out, but I just laugh and keep moving.

It's all good until, at the last second, and before it's too late to correct my trajectory, I skate over a big fucking divot in the ice.

"Shiiit!" I lose my footing and go down like a ton of bricks.

Pain immediately bursts through my ankle, and I begin screaming, "Noooo! God-fucking-dammit, you have got to be kidding me."

My teammates are laughing at first, until they skate over and see I'm serious and that I haven't gotten up.

"Hey, you okay, man?" Nolan asks grimly.

"What happened?" Benny asks.

Pointing down to my twisted foot, I grumble, "I think I may have just broken my fucking ankle."

10

0 FOR 2

AUBREY

When we arrive at the dress shop, I hand them the shipping slip for my wedding gown.

But to my dismay, the elderly sales lady at the counter has no idea what I'm talking about.

"What does that even mean?" I ask when she says she hasn't heard of any shipments coming in from Las Vegas. "Where is my dress, then?"

I'm feeling ill. I just knew something bad would happen. Now I won't sleep a wink, what with worrying about my missing gown.

"I gave explicit instructions to have it shipped to *this* address,"

I lament on a sigh.

The grumpy woman looks at my slip again.

"Hmm, I don't know," she mumbles. "I don't think it'll help, but I can check again if you'd like."

"Please," I mutter.

Huffing, like I'm wasting her time, she begins paging through the box of invoices for a second time.

Truth is, I don't hold out much hope. It's not going to magically appear.

Sure enough, once she's finished, she looks up and says, "I'm sorry, but I still don't see anything here, Ms. Shelburne."

"Can you check in the back maybe?" I plead. "The dress may have arrived and someone just forgot to take the paperwork out of the shipping box. It is only a little past noon. It could be back there and not checked in."

"Highly unlikely." She bristles. "As I told you, we received all of our shipments for the day. And I can assure you that if your dress was here at the shop, the documentation would be in with the inv—"

"Hey!" Lainey steps forward. "Not to be rude or anything, but this is my sister's wedding dress we're talking about. You can either check in the back right now, or let *me* do it."

"Lainey, my hero," I murmur as I place my arm around her slim waist.

The sales lady harrumphs, but scurries off, though not before uttering a disgruntled, "I'll be right back."

"Look at you, Miss Get Results," Eliza says to Lainey with an impressed nod once the saleswoman disappears to the back.

Tugging my sister in close to me, I kiss her cheek. "I love you. You know that, right?"

"Ah, I do know that. And I love you too, Aubs. That's why I always have your back."

"You do, don't you?"

"Yep." She nods proudly. "Whether strippers or a missing dress, I'm on it for you."

"You are," Eliza interjects, "sometimes even literally."

We all laugh at the fresh memory of Lainey taking down the strippers.

"Nolan really is lucky to have you," I tell her. "And I am too."

My sister actually blushes. "Aww, Aubrey."

Lainey is so loud and brash sometimes, but so shy and humble at others.

"You're such a contradiction," I tell her.

Winking at me, she says, "Nolan says the same thing. He claims that's what keeps things interesting with us." With a nudge, she adds, "If you know what I mean."

She winks and I roll my eyes. "Dear Lord, here we go."

Eliza asks, "Is this more sex talk?"

"You know it," I reply. "With Lainey, it's always sex, sex, and more sex."

"Sounds like life with Benny," Eliza remarks wistfully. "I swear he's insatiable."

Hell, I give up with these two. If you can't beat 'em, you may as well join them, right?

So I do.

"Yeah, Brent is pretty much insatiable, as well," I say. "Not that I'm complaining."

The stuffy sales lady returns and, having clearly overheard at least part of our conversation, shakes her head disapprovingly.

"She seems like she could use some dick," my sister whispers, a little on the loud side. "Maybe you should give her that extra Area 51 you brought along."

"Hey, not before I get mine," Eliza cries out.

We all look at each other and can't help but lose it on the spot.

Stuffy Sales Lady Who Clearly Needs Dick—her new name, by the way—is *not* amused.

In a chastising tone, she snaps, "Ladies, please. We run a classy, upscale establishment here."

That makes me so mad that I snap back, "Yeah, a classy, upscale establishment that loses people's wedding gowns!"

Just then the manager notices the ruckus and comes over to see what's going on.

After hearing about the missing dress, and checking for the invoice like it might magically appear, she dismisses Stuffy Sales Lady Who Clearly Needs Dick and begins apologizing profusely.

She's much nicer and promises to look into where my dress could be.

I conclude that she, unlike the other lady, must be getting a little something-something somewhere—either from a person or through self-satisfaction.

Hey, maybe I should give her the extra Area 51.

On the way home, I run that idea by the girls, and though they veto it, we have a good laugh imagining it.

"Hey, no one's getting one of those Area 51s until I get mine," Eliza warns.

"Okay, okay, I promise I'll dig through my luggage tonight. When I find the damn things, I'll put them on the dresser in our bedroom so I don't forget to give you yours."

"Cool," she replies. "But maybe leave mine there until I tell you I need it. I'd like to surprise Benny when the time is right and I don't want him running across it in our bedroom beforehand."

"Ooh, thanks for telling me that," I say. "And don't worry. Your Area 51 shall remain on the dresser till you say otherwise, m'dear."

"Thanks, Aubrey," she replies, laughing.

All in all, despite the setback at the dress shop, I'm in a really good mood by the time we return to the lake house.

But then I walk in and go upstairs, only to find Brent seated on our bed with his leg propped up.

"What the hell?" I cry out. "What happened?"

His ankle is swollen to about three times its normal size.

Whatever occurred, this is truly a disaster.

What could go wrong next?

Do I even want to know?

11

LET'S CALL THE WHOLE THING OFF

BRENT

"Oh, Brent…" Aubrey places her face in her hands and sobs. "Everything that can possibly go wrong *is* going wrong. First, my dress is MIA and now"—she looks up and gestures to my wrapped ankle—"you end up injured just going for a casual, fun skate. I don't know. Maybe we should just call the whole thing off."

"What?" I blurt out. "Cancel the wedding? No, sweetheart, you can't be serious."

Aubrey sighs. "We could always just run off and elope."

"Um…"

She glances down at my ankle and cries, "No, wait, that's out too. We can't run off when you can barely *walk*."

She chokes back another sob, and I wish I could jump up like I always do and go to her.

I can't, though, thanks to my damn wounded ankle.

We're in our bedroom, and I'm propped up on the bed. There's an ice pack resting on my wrapped injury in an attempt to reduce the crazy swelling.

Too bad it's not working.

Aubrey is seated on the edge of the bed, her face in her hands again.

Shit, she's still crying.

I do the only thing I'm able to do—I lean over and reach for her so I can pull her to me.

But even when I try that—*fuck me all to hell!*—pain shoots up my leg.

"Shit!" I crumple back against the pillows, wincing.

"Brent…" Aubrey crawls up into my arms. "This is so, so bad. What are we going to do?"

"Everything will be fine," I tell her in what I hope is a convincing tone. "The family doctor who made the emergency house call just before you guys got back said my ankle is just badly sprained. He left crutches for me to use for now, though he insists so long as I baby it, my ankle should be good as new in time for the wedding."

That just makes her cry harder.

"B-b-but we still can't get married. How can I stand at the altar not wearing my dream wedding gown?" She motions to her ripped jeans and tee and sobs, "I'll probably just be stuck wearing something bummy like this."

Crap, I need to cheer her up. This is going downhill fast.

I glance over to a chair where undergarments she brought along for the wedding night—a silky white bra, panties, and a garter with white stockings that are sexy as hell—lie draped over the back.

Truthfully, they were all I could think about before Aubrey returned. I can't wait to see them on her...and to strip them off her.

But for now, maybe I can make her smile with some witty commentary. Yeah, that should work.

Nodding to the lingerie, I playfully state, "Hey, you could always just wear that getup over there. I'd be cool with that."

She scoffs. "Of course you'd be okay with me wearing itty, bitty undergarments to the ceremony."

I hold her closer and joke, "Hey, why the hell not?"

She smacks my arm. "Brent, be serious."

"Oh, come on. Think about it. You'd certainly have everyone's full attention. And isn't that what every bride wants?"

She finally laughs, and I'm glad my silly attempt to lighten things up is finally working.

"Brent, you're so bad," she says.

"That's right. I'm so bad that I'm actually good, babe."

Laughing even harder, she says, "Stop it."

I rest my chin on her head. "Okay, sweetheart, I'll behave."

We sit quietly then, till out of the blue, she looks up and says, "Oh my God, I just thought of something hilarious."

I rub her back. "What's that, Aubs?"

"Didn't you tell me that your aunt on your dad's side is, like, super stuffy?"

I let out a chuckle. "Aunt Gertrude? Yeah, you could say she's a tad uptight."

"Well then, could you just imagine her reaction if I actually wore lingerie and nothing else for the wedding?"

I laugh. "She'd surely have a coronary on the spot. You know, I really don't think she's ever had sex. It's probably too 'messy' for her."

Aubrey peers up at me, brow furrowed. "But she has twin boys, right?"

"Uh-huh. Ricky and Ronny are adopted, though," I explain.

"Ah, got it. Still, I'm sure she's gotten some sex somewhere at some point."

"Maybe," I say. "But heaven knows she sure could use some now."

Just then I remember something else about Aunt Gertrude, and it's important.

"About those boys, Aubrey…"

"What about them?" she asks.

"When they're around, be sure you lock our bedroom door. They're only eight, but those twins have no respect for privacy. They literally get into *everything*. They were here at the lake house one time and grabbed two hockey sticks from my room. We heard them out in the hallway, and when we went to see what was going on, they were beating the living hell out of each other with the sticks."

"Charming," Aubrey says sarcastically. "I'll be sure to let Eliza and Lainey know to lock their bedroom doors too."

"Good idea. Those kids are truly out of control."

With Aubrey in a better mood, we lie there and talk about a lot of non-wedding-related shit, like how everyone is getting along and having a nice time.

"I'm glad our wave of bad luck hasn't spread to anyone else," Aubrey states.

"Yeah, me too."

Suddenly chewing her lip, she makes a face.

"What now?" I ask.

She sighs. "I was just thinking that maybe we should stay in tonight. I was originally planning to suggest we all go out for a big fancy dinner in town. But with you hurt and misfortune following us, it might be safer to stay in."

I can't disagree, plus I should stay off my bad ankle, so I reply, "Okay. Why don't we order in a bunch of pizzas?"

"That sounds perfect, Brent. And afterward we can just hang out. Maybe even have a few drinks. Well," she clarifies, "not Benny, since he no longer drinks. But I sure could use some alcohol after the day I just had."

"Hell," I laugh, "I could use some too."

Aubrey rolls away from me so she can stand. "I better go downstairs and get everyone up to speed," she says.

"Okay, babe."

After she leaves, I rake my fingers through my dark hair.

Shit, I hope the doctor's right and I'm okay for the wedding, since Aubrey sure will be disappointed if I have to hobble down the aisle on crutches.

12

DICK-MEASURING CONTEST IS ON

AUBREY

The pizza is good, but the drinks afterward are even better.

My sister, calling on her former cocktail-waitressing skills, whips up an assortment of summery frozen beverages, things like piña coladas, strawberry daiquiris, and frozen margaritas.

Mmmm...

She also insists on serving them to us.

I suspect that's so we don't see how much alcohol she's added to each frothy concoction. This way she can get us good and drunk.

That's fine with me, as we're all staying in, meaning no one will be driving.

What's extra sweet and thoughtful, though, is that Lainey makes a special nonalcoholic batch of drinks just for Benny. She tells him this way he can be part of the festivities and not have to worry about messing with his sobriety.

Benny tells Lainey he really appreciates that, as does Eliza.

When my sister brings in round three on a serving tray, Nolan, naughty as always, and probably a little buzzed by now, remarks, "Babe, too bad you didn't pack your sexy bar wench outfit. It would've been perfect for tonight."

I can't tell if he means for her waitressing for us…or for him later.

Lainey's bar wench uniform is pretty sexy, consisting of a black pair of thigh-high boots, a short black skirt, a flouncy white blouse, and a corset to wear overtop that makes her boobs look absolutely huge.

Nolan, of course, loves it.

Lainey stops by his recliner and, with her free hand, smacks him on the arm.

"Nolan, don't be silly. I don't even know where I put that old thing."

Nolan stares up at her, appearing confused.

"Sure you do," he says. "You wore it for me one night about a month ago. You haven't forgotten about that, have you? We were role-playing. I was supposed to be a knight from the Middle Ages, and I'd captured you, the fair maiden—"

"Ugh, that's enough." I cover my ears. "TMI, TMI. I don't want to hear another word."

As it is, I know enough about their sex life from Lainey. The last thing I want now are images of them "role-playing" bouncing around in my brain.

Though, come to think of it, I bet Brent would really like if I suggested such a thing for us to try.

Hmm, Brent as a knight and me as a fair maiden... This is totally doable.

I could be in distress and he has to rescue me. I'd then feel compelled to reward him, right? But, oh my goodness, fair maiden-me has never been with a man.

I glance over at Brent and swallow hard.

Knowing me well, he raises a questioning brow.

Yeah, I think I'll ask Lainey if I can borrow that outfit when we get back to Vegas.

Just then, Lainey, noticing my exchange with Brent, and knowing me too damn well too, rolls her eyes my way.

"You are such a little hypocrite, Aubrey."

"What?"

She tsks, "Pretending to be a prude when all along you're over there thinking about how much you'd like role-playing with Brent."

"Hey, I'm not a prude," I cry out, attempting to defend my pervert integrity.

"Are too," she chides.

She's still passing out drinks, so I snatch mine from her forcefully.

"Am not," I murmur.

"Then prove it," she says.

Ooh, a challenge!

"Okay, I will."

I look around.

Wow, everyone is watching our exchange. I better come up with something good.

The first thing that pops into my mind is the conversation we had at the male revue.

Oh, you know the one.

Proudly, I announce, "We're going to have that dick-measuring contest we talked about at my bachelorette party. Then you'll see that I'm no prude, especially because *I'm* going to be the deciding judge!"

"Dick-measuring contest?" Brent asks, looking at me like I've lost my mind. "What the hell are you talking about?"

Eliza, of course, over by Benny, is cracking up.

Benny, the only sober one at this point, eyes me warily.

Nolan is too busy staring at Lainey's jean-clad ass to offer any commentary.

Figures.

Meanwhile, my sister is gawking at me in disbelief.

"Just how much have you had to drink, Aubrey?" she asks.

"Enough," I reply, giggling, "that the dick-measuring contest is on, bitch."

13

BUT YOU DON'T EVEN HAVE A DICK

BRENT

I have no idea what Aubrey's going on about, but the girls sure seem to. They're frighteningly pumped for this... uh... "dick-measuring" contest.

Turning to my wild and crazy wife-to-be, I murmur, "Uh, last time I checked, babe, you don't have a dick. So how's this supposed to work?"

"It's not a contest for me and the girls, silly man," she says, rolling her pretty turquoise eyes. "We're going to measure you and the guys.'"

I chuckle, like *yeah right*. "You think so, huh? And what else did you just say to everyone? *You're* planning to be the deciding judge?"

I level her with an I-don't-think-so glare, but she naturally ignores me.

Instead, she states smugly, "Yep, I am."

That's when I lose it.

"Over my dead body you are!" I roar. "My soon-to-be wife is not going anywhere near these two jerk-offs' junk."

I gesture angrily to Nolan and Benny, and Nolan says, "Jerk-off, huh? Funny, but that's how I plan to get ready for this contest. A little preliminary stroking the ole trouser trout should do the trick, right?"

Nolan goes fishing once and now half his jokes are aquatic-related. *Heaven help us.*

In any case, I know he's being his usual smartass self. Still, I feel compelled to shoot him a wicked glare.

Aubrey, meanwhile, is going on and on about how this will prove to her sister once and for all that she's not a prude.

"Ah, babe, I think there are better ways to make your point," I remark.

"Yes, by measuring cocks," she tells me.

Okay, seriously, if she thinks I'm cool with her holding a tape measure up to my teammates' hard dicks, which could easily lead to incidental touching, she is off her rocker.

"Are you fucking nuts?" I grind out.

Lainey, zoning in on the "nuts" part of my comment—no

surprise there—muses, "Hey, maybe we should measure those too. You know, to find out whose sack is the biggest."

Whaaat?

"You Shelburne women are fucking loco," I murmur. Then, pointing at Nolan, I add, "You best rein in your woman, my friend."

He laughs. "Are you serious? There's no reining Lainey in, Brent. Not Aubrey, either. Haven't you realized that by now? Remember how we thought we'd tamed them? Well, I've finally come to the conclusion it's just not possible. Embrace it, man, make peace with yourself."

Hmm, he may have a point. Several points, actually.

But I'm not giving in on this dick thing. Hell, I haven't even agreed to have my own member measured. Not that I think I'd lose or anything.

Fuck, no. I *know* my cock is king.

Benny, I'm sure due to him being the only sober one, comes up with a sensible compromise.

"How about if we just let our partners measure us individually...and privately?"

"Or the guys could measure each other," Eliza interjects.

We all look at each other and shout a collective, "No!"

"Sorry, but I'm not getting anywhere near either of their penises," I snort.

Nolan and Benny wholeheartedly agree, and that wacky idea

is thankfully scrapped.

"Okay, so back to our partners measuring us," Benny begins.

"But then there could be cheating," Aubrey objects.

Is my girl really that interested in keeping this goofy contest on the up-and-up? No pun intended. Or does she actually maybe want to check out some other cocks?

Shit, I better follow up on that later. Maybe I'm not keeping her completely satisfied. I might need to up my game.

"Everyone just has to promise to be truthful," Lainey says.

"So, like, this is on the honor system?" Eliza clarifies.

"Yes." Lainey then warns, "No cheating, though…or else."

Hell, I don't even want to know what her "or else" could be, nor do I care to find out.

Remember, the Shelburne women are crazy. And the last thing I need is more "crazy" on my dick.

14

I BETTER GET HIM HARDER THAN I EVER HAVE

AUBREY

With the dick-measuring contest parameters set, we all disperse to our respective bedrooms.

Once I have Brent alone in ours and he's positioned how I want him—leaning back against a slew of pillows on the bed—I roll back my shoulders and start juking and jiving around the room.

Hey, a girl's got to loosen up, right?

"Brent," I say, bouncing on my toes. "I know your ankle's hurt and all, but that should have no effect on your cock. If we just relax and go with it, I think we got this."

He looks at me like I've lost my mind. And then he shakes

his head.

"What the hell are you doing, Aubrey? This isn't a *Rocky* reenactment. We're having a dick-measuring contest, not prepping for a boxing match. My dick's not fighting anyone."

"Ahh, and that's where you're wrong," I counter. "Your dick is going up against two of your teammates' peens. And from what I've been hearing, they're no slouches in the size department."

"That is info I so do not need to know," he states wearily.

"Hey." I snap my fingers. "Pay attention here, stay sharp. We're in it to win it, damn it." I roll my head, stretching out my neck. "And in order to accomplish that, I'm going to have to get you harder than I ever have before."

How can he argue with that?

He doesn't; he just shuts his damn mouth.

Yeah, that's what I thought.

Crawling up on the bed, I shove him back into the pillows, commanding, "Now relax."

"Ooh, Aubrey…" He laughs. "I think I like this demanding version of you."

"Ha." I whip my shirt up over my head and toss it aside. "You ain't seen nothin' yet, bud."

He smiles. And then, nodding down to his lap, he informs me, "Babe, I'm already getting hard. I think you're right. We are so going to win this."

Unclasping my bra, I let my breasts spill out as I murmur,

"Oh, we are, Brent. We are."

With my shirt and bra abandoned to the floor, I set aside the cloth measuring tape from Lainey. She had a bunch of them in her purse and passed one out to each couple before we dispersed.

Hmm, like she didn't plan all along for this to happen.

Ha! Well, it's on now.

I slide my shorts and panties down my legs and shimmy out of them.

"I think I should be completely naked," I say to Brent.

Again, there's no argument from him. He not only agrees, he starts eyeing me hungrily with those whiskey-colored eyes.

Good start.

After skimming my hands up and down my body in a teasing manner, I start playing with my breasts, until my nipples are hard and erect.

"Fuck, babe," Brent says roughly, the bulge in his pants growing larger and larger.

Smiling seductively, I lean forward and unbuckle his belt. "Pants and underwear off," I order.

Brent complies in about five seconds flat.

"Wow, that was fast," I remark, smirking, "especially for someone who's injured."

"I'm just going along with your demands," he replies. "And for the record, nothing really hurts right now, anyway."

"I bet," I say.

Brent's in charge so often in our bed that I'm not surprised he likes this turnabout of play.

I generally enjoy him being the boss—when it comes to sex, that is—but I can't deny taking charge now and again sure is fun.

"Okay," I say slowly as I decide what to order him to do next.

I'm getting pretty hot and bothered myself so it's hard to think clearly.

"Hmm," I begin, at last. "I think I'm going to play with my clit now. And you get to be a good boy and watch."

"Aubrey, shit." Brent's dick twitches.

Lifting my leg up and over him, placing my foot flat on the bed, I nod to my wet-as-fuck pussy and ask, "Do you like the view?"

"I fucking love it, Aubrey."

Unexpectedly, he lifts up and runs his tongue along my slit.

"Unh…wait. I'm supposed to be working on you," I say shakily.

He stops. "I know, but you know how much I love tasting you. Let me make you come first. Okay, Aubs? Watching you fall apart will have me so ready to explode that I'll be at my absolute hardest."

It's true—if Brent's on the verge, he'll be freaking huge.

How can I say no to that? It's like a double win.

Nodding rapidly, I agree.

Having been given the go-ahead, Brent returns to licking and lapping my folds, spreading me wide and doing his thing. Pretty soon his dick is harder than I've ever seen it.

"Ah, Brent," I gasp, my eyes practically rolling back in my head with how good what he's doing feels. "I, uh, I think we should stop for a sec and get in a quick measurement."

He peers up at me, his lips wet from my juices, as he says, "You sure about that, babe?"

I nod. "Uh-huh."

In the fog of impending orgasm, I fumble for the tape measure. Once I finally have it in my hand, I stretch it taut and measure Brent from base to tip.

"Wow," I marvel, "you're even bigger than I thought."

Brent preens. "Why, thank you, Aubrey."

He gains another tenth of an inch from my compliment.

"Good boy," I murmur, patting his thigh. "Your dick clearly likes flattery."

"It would seem so," he agrees, laughing.

With the number recorded in my head—I mean, shit, how could I forget *that* tally for a cock length?—I toss the tape measure aside.

And then I climb astride all nine-point-one inches of Brent Oliver and go for the ride of my life.

15

NUMBERS ARE IN AND WE HAVE A WINNER!

BRENT

"What do we get if we win?" Benny asks as he plops down on the big cushy chair to my right.

"Blow jobs from all the girls?" Nolan, seated over on the sofa, asks, raising a brow.

Good thing he's not close enough for me to smack him. Like Aubrey would ever agree to touch him. And like I'd go for something so stupid.

"You're such an ass." I glare over at my unruly teammate. "You fucking wish."

"Dude, that's so not cool," Benny tells Nolan with a did-you-really-just-say-that eye roll.

Sufficiently cowed, Nolan relents. "Okay, okay, I'm sorry. I was only joking."

"That better have just been a joke," I grumble, still feeling irritated with him.

We've reconvened in the living room. Well, the boys and I have. The ladies all wanted to "freshen up" before we got down to the results.

I have to laugh at that one. Everyone ended up fucking like Aubs and I. I'm not surprised, as that getting-ready-to-measure shit was far too hot.

I have to commend Lainey—the measuring contest was a stellar idea.

Speaking of the little devilette, she walks into the living room, looking happy and satisfied.

When I pull her aside to tell her I really fucking liked her idea, she smiles smugly.

"Thanks, Brent," she says. "I knew it'd turn out to be a lot of fun."

She's not kidding.

I notice then that she's holding a slip of paper in her hand.

Ha, that makes me laugh.

Guess she and Nolan felt compelled to record his measurement by writing it down.

Was it so unimpressive that you thought you'd forget? I consider saying.

But I don't.

After losing this contest, which Nolan surely will with me involved, they're bound to feel crappy enough.

Aubrey comes into the room next, along with Eliza. I notice both girls, and Lainey, are wearing black running shorts and black and red Wolves tees.

"Did you ladies all plan to dress alike, or have we officially entered mind-hive territory here?" I ask, chuckling.

"We planned it," Aubrey replies. "We wanted to let you guys know that no matter what the results are, we're all still a team here."

"Aw, babe…" I reach over and pull her onto my lap.

We start kissing because, damn, I always want my lips on this girl in some capacity.

But, of course, the gang starts razzing us and I know this tender moment won't last.

"Enough already," Nolan grumps.

Someone throws a decorative pillow from the sofa at us, probably him.

"Get a room!" another person shouts.

"They were just in a room, hon."

That's Benny, meaning the first comment was from Eliza.

"Looks like they need to go back," Lainey chimes in. "Maybe Brent didn't do it right the first time."

Her snide remark is enough to garner my attention, and thus

slam the brakes on Aubs and my make-out session.

Leaning back, I point to my soon-to-be sister-in-law and say, "Hey, let's get one thing straight, right here, right now. I definitely did do it right the first time." I look up at my girl and add, "Isn't that right, Aubrey?"

"Damn straight." She leans down and touches her lips to mine. "You sure did, Brent."

And just to stick it to Lainey, we play tongue hockey again until everyone starts groaning.

"That'll fix you fuckers," I murmur once we finally break apart.

It may have been Lainey who pissed me off, but the others were all commenting too.

"Are we going to announce the numbers or not?" I state.

It's time to get down to business.

"Yeah, let's do it," Benny replies, nodding. "I'm ready."

Lainey holds up her slip of paper and smugly states, "I think we should clap for Nolan now since I already know he definitely won."

The other girls grumble over that one. And then Lainey is pissed too, mad that Aubrey and Eliza didn't officially "record" their results.

"How are we supposed to know you're telling the truth?" Lainey accuses, eyeing them suspiciously.

Aubrey protests, "Same goes for you. Just because you wrote

something down doesn't make it official or anything."

Lainey concedes, "Yeah, but what if you forgot the specific final figure?"

"Trust me." Aubrey squeezes my thigh since she's still on my lap. "There's no way I could ever forget Brent's measurement… like ever."

She's just the best.

"I should marry you," I murmur. And then, smacking my forehead, I exclaim, "Wait, I'm already doing that."

Aubrey snorts, "Brent, you're so silly sometimes."

Eliza chimes in then, though not in regards to me. She's too busy defending her memorization skills.

"Benny's number in my head is perfectly accurate," she says. "And for the record, he beat all your dick lengths so you may as well give it up now."

"We'll see about that," I murmur.

"Can we just get to the numbers, already?" Nolan grumbles.

"Yes, let's," I say.

Aubrey, straightening up, but remaining in my lap, asks everyone, "Who wants to go first?"

Eliza raises her hand. "Ooh, me, me. I'll go first."

"All righty then." Aubrey clears her throat. "How long is Benny Perry's dick?"

Preening, Eliza states, "Eight and a half inches."

"Ha," I bark out.

Aubrey smacks me. "Wait your turn, Brent. I think Lainey should go next with Nolan's result."

You can tell she really wants me to beat Nolan.

And hell, I do too.

Lainey, agreeing to go next, makes a big production in preparing to read out Nolan's number.

Unfolding her slip of paper, she clears her throat, pauses, then finally announces, "Nolan Solvenson came in at…drum roll, please…nine inches on the nose."

"Oh my God, Brent!" Aubrey wraps her arms around me and squeals, "We won, we won!"

I feel pretty smug that, though not by much, I've beaten both my teammates. I guess it's just my competitive nature to always want to win at everything.

Raising a brow while peering up at my girl, I say, "Want to go back to the bedroom and celebrate?"

Just like how I feel about kissing her, I can never get enough of sticking my dick in her too—all nine-point-one inches of it.

Aubrey nods, but everyone makes her announce my dick size before we disappear to our room.

"Okay, okay," she says. "Brent Oliver came in at an impressive nine-point-one inches."

"Ah, I was so close," Nolan laments, bowing his head.

"I demand a redo," Benny yells. "I was losing my sexy thoughts mojo when Eliza finally pulled out the tape measure."

"That's because *you* pulled out too soon," Eliza retorts. "I told you to wait until you were ready to erupt."

Lainey turns to Nolan. "Yeah, and I should've done that thing I do with my tongue before we measured. You know, that one you like so much? I bet doing that would've added the extra bump we needed to beat damn Brent."

I wince. "Jesus, God, enough with all the detail already. Last thing I care to have stuck in my head are images of their dicks." I gesture to Benny and Nolan.

"Really," Nolan says. "He has a point."

"For sure," Benny concurs.

With the numbers in, we finally all agree that it was a close one. Everyone did well.

"On any given Sunday," Benny laments. "You know, that means we all had a chance to win."

Aubrey rolls her eyes, and I remind Benny that it's actually Saturday.

"Oh, yeah, that's right," he says.

"Well, at least it was a fun contest," declares Eliza.

No one can argue with that.

But, of course, Nolan has to snark, "Yeah, we should do it again sometime."

He's totally joking, but Lainey jumps all over it like he's dead serious.

"Hey, we absolutely should do this again," she says. "But this time, let's make it a widest girth contest!"

That's when we all groan and throw a barrage of decorative pillows at her.

16

BENNY'S SPECIAL-ORDER DONUTS

AUBREY

'm kind of glad the dick-measuring contest is behind us. That means we can all get back to focusing on why we're in Minnesota—for the freaking wedding, people!

Speaking of our upcoming nuptials, Brent and I spend the morning working on our vows. Turns out we have some very lovely things to say about each other, which is good since we're about to become husband and wife.

I tell him as much and he replies, "You know what? I never thought I could be this excited about getting married. But I am. I can't wait to make you my wife."

"I'm pumped about the wedding too," I share. "Now if

everything could just come together."

He knows I'm talking about the setbacks as of late. There's so much more than vows to worry about.

And I'm right to be concerned.

The next day arrives, Monday, and I discover that my dress is *still* not in.

Nor is it at the bridal shop on Tuesday…or Wednesday.

I'm not panicking, you're panicking.

Yeah, right.

Truth is, by Thursday, I'm completely freaking out. I mean, crap, the wedding is only nine days away. That's not enough time to have a new gown made. Not to mention, I love my dress. I don't want to wear anything else.

But it's not just the missing dress that's weighing me down. Worrying about Brent is keeping me up night after night. His ankle is healing, sure, and he no longer needs the crutches to get around, but he's still in a lot of pain.

"I'm really concerned about Brent," I share with my sister as we're driving away, empty-handed once again, from the bridal shop.

"The wedding is next Saturday," I go on, "and I'm not even sure he'll be able to walk down the aisle without limping."

"Pfft," Lainey snorts from over in the passenger seat. "That's the least of your worries, Aubrey. Brent can at least hobble to the altar in his nicely tailored tux. You, on the other hand, you'll be lucky to not have to walk down the aisle in jeans and a T-shirt."

"I know. I was just saying that exact same thing to Brent the other day." I shake my head. "This is truly awful, Lainey."

"I'm sorry this is happening to you," my sister says, her tone heartfelt.

As we continue driving through town, I focus on the various shops, reading each of their quaint little names to myself. I need something to distract myself from my troubles or I may start crying.

And never stop.

As I'm checking out the stores, I spot a cute little bohemian donut shop named Karma Kreme.

"Ooh, let's stop in and pick up some donuts," I say to Lainey, pointing over to the pretty purple sign.

"Planning on dealing with your wedding problems with carbs and sugar loading?" Lainey asks.

I shrug as I turn into the Karma Kreme parking lot.

"It works for Benny, right?"

My sister replies, "True. And speaking of donut-loving Benjamin Perry, you better buy extra donuts if we go in here. Otherwise, he'll scarf down *all* ours."

I laugh and state, "Good call."

I then remember that Brent's parents and his stuffy Aunt Gertrude—along with her twin sons, Ricky and Ronny—are coming over to the lake house later tonight for a visit.

I share this with Lainey and add, "You know what? With that many people in the house, I think we better just go with a couple dozen to be safe."

"Maybe make that three," she says.

"I agree."

After we're parked, we go into the donut shop.

I am immediately enchanted, as it's freaking adorable inside the place. Not only are there funky paintings adorning the eccentric aqua and yellow walls, but viney spider plants are spindling and trailing everywhere. Bob Marley is on in the background and people are seated on purple sofas. They're chatting, reading, and working on their laptops.

Some, though, are simply eating donuts—which, by the way, look delicious.

The whole vibe just screams: this is a cool place to hang out.

"Wow, I love it here," Lainey murmurs as we walk to the display cases in the rear of the store.

"It really is adorable," I agree.

That adorability quotient almost shoots through the roof when we reach the display cases and discover the cutest specialty donuts…like, ever.

"Oh my God, Aubs," Lainey cries out. "Look at those sweet donut puppies!"

"Aww, those are awesome. And check it out. They have kitten donuts too."

"So sweet," she coos. "There are bunnies in there too."

"Damn, too bad Chloe's not in town yet. She'd love those."

Chloe has a pet rabbit named Jackie that she and Dylan dote on all the time. It's a spoiled little thing. I can only imagine how pampered their child will be once she's born.

I nudge Lainey and we continue to *ooh* and *aah* over all the specialty creations. There are so many interestingly shaped donuts, not just the cute animal ones. Some are designed and decorated to look like flowers and others are replica rockets and stars.

"Whoever creates these is really talented," I remark.

Lainey agrees. "Yeah, I bet kids really like those rocket- and star-shaped ones."

"Hmm, maybe I should buy a few then for Aunt Gertrude's boys. Brent mentioned once that they're really into *Star Wars*."

Lainey nods. "Oh, then those would be a hit, for sure."

"Okay. We'll buy some of those, plus a few other designs."

"Cool."

Just then a cute girl with dreads comes over to wait on us.

"May I help you, ladies?" she asks with a cheery grin.

"Yes." I nod. "I'm going to need a few dozen donuts, please."

"You've come to the right place," she deadpans.

I laugh. "Clearly."

Once I tell her exactly how many we want, she grabs three boxes and begins lining them with wax paper.

"What would you like to start with?" she asks once she's done.

I point inside the case. "Definitely some of those rockets and stars donuts."

The girl works on boxing up donuts, but hesitates at one point, eyeing me curiously like maybe she just now recognized me.

Softly, she says, "Hey, not to invade your privacy or anything, but may I ask you a question?"

"Yeah, sure."

"Are you, by chance, Brent Oliver's fiancée?"

I smile. I'm used to being recognized by now, and I always try to handle it graciously. It really is an honor to be associated with Brent.

"I am, yes," I confirm.

"I thought so," she says. And then, after a long pause, she adds, "It's just that everyone in town knows you're getting married next weekend. I guess you could say we've all been keeping tabs on the various players coming in. Like, just the other day, Benny Perry stopped in the store. We knew immediately who he was. We were all excited when he placed a big custom specialty donut order."

"Oh he did, huh?" I murmur.

She nods. "Yes. And it's actually ready to go. If you'd like, I can give you his donuts to take back with you. I mean, it's up to you. But this way he wouldn't have to make a special trip into town or anything. Plus, it's already paid for."

"Sure, okay." I nod. "We can do that."

Hmm, now I'm curious as to what kind of specialty donut order Benny placed. So I decide to ask for details.

But the girl just shrugs. "I'm sorry, but I don't really know. I was here at the store that day he came in, but I didn't take the actual order. The baker himself came out from the back and talked to him personally." She pauses, then adds, "Come to think of it, it was all really secretive. I guess Mr. Perry wanted to keep his special order on the down-low for some reason."

"Interesting," I murmur. "I'm sure he did. Benny kind of has a donut addiction that we all like to tease him about. I bet that's why."

"Oh," the girl replies. "Yes. That must've been the reason, then."

Lainey asks how many donuts Benny ordered, and the girl says, "Two dozen."

I let her know that we can definitely take the order to Benny.

"But," I say, turning to Lainey, "we need to keep picking out donuts of our own for Brent's family."

She nods. "For sure. Benny will, no doubt, want all his donuts for his donut-loving self."

"You think he can really eat twenty-four donuts?" I snort.

Lainey shrugs. "I don't know, but probably."

I think about how we're talking Benny here and sigh. "Yeah, you're right."

We go on to choose an assortment of cute animal-shaped confections and several flower donuts to go along with the already-picked rockets and stars. All told, once we're done, we walk out of the donut shop with Benny's two dozen, plus three dozen of our own.

With so many, I put Lainey in charge of keeping the donut orders separated.

"Maybe you should mark them," I suggest once we're back in the car.

"No need," Lainey says. "I know whose are whose."

"All righty then, if you say so." I blow out a breath. "But it's up to you to explain to Benny what happened if someone eats his freaking special mystery batch."

Of course, Lainey brushes that off. She's too busy musing, "Hmm, I still wonder what kind of donuts he had designed."

"I'm actually really curious too," I confess. "Too bad the boxes are all taped up. And, look, there's even string tied around them."

"We could always try to lift an edge and peek in," Lainey offers.

But I tell her I don't think that's a good idea. "The boxes will end up all bent up and he'll know we were snooping."

"Yeah, yeah, you're right," she concedes.

Still, I am dying of curiosity.

It's then that I decide to "accidentally" mix up the orders when Lainey's not looking. This way we can see what kind of donuts Benny had made when we open the boxes to serve the donuts to our guests tonight.

Hmm, I bet Benny had something really adorable designed for Eliza.

Or maybe he had some kind of cute wedding-themed donuts created for all of us to gorge on.

Yeah, I bet that's what's in his boxes.

As I'm driving away from the bakery, I'm already imagining cute, little white church-shaped donuts with really tall steeples, like the church Brent and I are to be married in.

And all I can think is, *Aww, this is going to be so sweet.*

FAMILY NIGHT

BRENT

So my folks are coming over to the lake house tonight. Normally I'd be pretty amped about that, as I get along well with them, but they're bringing my prissy Aunt Gertrude *and* her monster twins.

Er, I mean her nice sons, Ricky and Ronny.

Damn, I can't even lie.

Those kids are the worst.

I've already warned Aubrey and the rest of the gang, but no one is prepared for when the demon seeds come in the door.

Like whirling dervishes, in no less than two minutes flat, they're running around the house like they own the place, chasing and smacking each other.

"Oh, dear," Aunt Gertrude laments as she wrings her hands. "Boys, stop it. Stop with this foolishness right now."

She turns to me and, in a totally serious voice, says, "They're usually much better-behaved when visiting people. I just don't know what's gotten into them tonight."

Riiight…sure they are. I remember the hockey stick battle.

The boys run by us in the entry hall, ignoring their mother's admonishments. They deviate to avoid her by clambering up the stairs leading up to the living room.

I sigh.

I'd like to say something to get them to stop running around, but I don't want to cause any trouble. Aunt Gertrude is freaking hair-trigger sensitive when it comes to her "babies."

Though I may have to speak up at some point, as I now hear them scampering around upstairs, probably terrorizing my houseguests.

Aubrey is standing next to me, listening to the racket. Leaning in, she whispers, "Good God. They really are monsters, aren't they?"

"Told you they were bad," I mumble, so Aunt Gertrude doesn't hear.

My parents, meanwhile, are just shaking their heads.

Benny, who was up in the living room with the rest of the crew, waiting for us to come up, jogs down the stairs to where we're clearly at an impasse.

Yeah, we haven't made it any farther, not with the evil twins on their rampage.

"Hey, I heard the commotion down here," he begins. "And I also think I caught a blur of some small people running by me in the living room just a minute ago."

"Sorry about that," I murmur, feeling frustrated.

Benny, noticing my distress, says, "Hey, if you'd like, I can set up your Xbox down in the basement family room. You still have that it, right?"

"I do," I confirm.

"Well then, let me get the kids started on a game. Maybe that'll keep them out of your hair for a while and you can entertain your guests."

"Yeah, but you're a guest too," I say quietly. "You shouldn't have to babysit."

He waves his hand. "Aw, hell, I don't mind."

Benny is truly amazing with kids. I mean, shit, he's fantastic with Eliza's little daughter, Ava.

Still, I should warn him that he's about to have his hands full with Ricky and Ronny.

I don't get the chance, though. Aunt Gertrude, who I fully expected to nix the Xbox idea, is totally on board.

I look at her, and she's smiling and nodding at Benny.

Wow, this is a first.

Touching my teammate's arm, Aunt Gertrude gushes, "That's such a wonderful idea, you big, strapping young man. I'm sure the boys will love the Xbox. They're really into video games."

Jesus, I think she's taken a liking to my teammate.

Good thing Eliza has nothing to worry about. Even if he weren't attached, and even back in his wild days, Benny would never hook up with my forty-something, skeletal-looking aunt.

First, she's far too uptight, not to mention judgmental as hell. But also, Benny likes his women much younger and with a little curve to them. Not to mention, it'd take a *really* special man to deal with the double devil spawn on a regular basis.

And just then, like I've summoned the small demons just with my thoughts, devil spawn number one, Ronny, runs back downstairs.

I resist the urge to trip him as he ambles past. Good thing Benny is a much more reasonable man.

He catches Ronny by the arm, corralling him easily. "Hey, hey, hold up there for a minute, kid."

Ronny struggles for all of about ten seconds, until he realizes his plight.

Yeah, bud, there's no getting away from big Benny. Just ask any opposing player about that.

Normally my aunt would start huffing and puffing—how dare anyone touch her precious babies—but because it's Benny, she just smiles over at him all googly like.

Heaven help us.

"It's so nice to see a forceful man take charge," Aunt Gertrude states dreamily.

"Oh, uh"—Benny, obviously catching on that she's into him, begins to blush—"I, um, I was just trying to catch one of your boys to ask him if he and his brother would like to play those video games I mentioned."

"Video games, video games, yes, yes, yes! Hey, Ricky," Ronny screams up the stairs. "Get your butt down here."

His brother races down the stairs, and after he hears Benny's idea, he says, "Yeah, maybe. What kind of games do you have? Nothing lame, right?"

"I have *Call of Duty*," I reply. "That's hardly lame."

How dare these brats question my game library!

They say then that they love *Call of Duty*, which I figured they would.

Benny, poor guy, now has the task of herding them down to the basement.

Too bad there are no shackles and chains down there. We could just lock them up.

Just kidding!

"Sorry, dude," I murmur to Benny as he walks by with his charges in tow.

"Not a problem," he murmurs back. "I volunteered, remember?"

"Still, I owe you one."

He claps me on the back. "Just go spend some time with your family, man."

Now that Ricky and Ronny are preoccupied, I do exactly that.

Once we're finally all convened in the living room, I introduce everyone. My parents have already met my teammates, of course, but Lainey and Eliza are new to them.

And, well, everyone is new to Aunt Gertrude.

I gave the gang a heads-up earlier to watch their language and steer away from risqué topics. My parents are pretty cool with things like that, but Aunt Gertrude... Well, she's a different story.

Everyone remember to stick to safe topics. Yay!

See, there's nothing to worry about. This night is going to be a success.

We talk mostly about wedding stuff and also about what we've all been up to at the lake house. We leave out the dick-measuring contest, for obvious reasons. Even my über-cool parents might wonder about me on that one. Though I bet my dad would be really proud that I won.

"You're a chip off the old block, son," I imagine him saying.

Ugh, wait, no.

That makes me think about my dad's dick, and dudes, that's a hard pass.

Disturbed, I shake my head and make a sour face.

Aubrey, seated next to me on the sofa, notices and touches my thigh.

"Is everything okay?" she asks softly.

"Everything is fine, babe. My train of thought just got derailed there for a minute."

"Care to share?"

"Good God, no." The last thing I want is for Aubrey to be thinking about my dad's dick too.

She continues to peer over at me, until she finally says, "Whatever, Brent. Maybe we should just move on and offer our guests some refreshments."

"That's a great idea, babe," I reply, relieved.

Aubrey stands up and announces that we have donuts and coffee for everyone. My family is excited—sugar addicts!—while Lainey jumps up to help.

Eliza starts to volunteer to also assist in getting the refreshments, but Aunt Gertrude quickly cuts her off.

"No, no, you just stay there, missy. I'll help instead."

Aunt Gertrude's been really snippy with Eliza since she found out she's with Benny.

Women.

I shake my head, chuckling.

Eliza, gracious as always, says to Aunt Gertrude, "That's fine. Be my guest."

I shoot her a discreet thank-you nod, but she just shrugs,

taking it all in stride. She and Benny really are perfect for one another. They're just so damn laid back.

While Aubrey, Lainey, and my aunt head down to the kitchen, I look around and breathe a sigh of relief. My parents are talking with Nolan, and there's been no further commotion with the twins. Guess Benny has them fully engaged in the game.

Wow, I can't believe this family night is going so incredibly well.

But just then, all calmness is shattered when a blood-curdling scream rings out from downstairs in the kitchen.

What the…?

"Oh, dear Lord, what kind of awful donuts are those?" I hear Aunt Gertrude exclaiming. "You young people nowadays are just sick, sick, sick."

NOPE, NOT CHURCHES

AUBREY

There are multiple things happening at once.

And none of them are good.

For starters, Aunt Gertrude opens a box of Benny's special-order donuts, and based on the contents, which I take a peek in at, she's naturally aghast.

Oops, guess I shouldn't have shuffled around the boxes, after all.

After screaming like a serial killer just walked into the house, Aunt Gertrude shouts, "Oh, dear Lord, what kind of awful donuts are those? You young people nowadays are just sick, sick, sick."

Lainey looks into the box and starts laughing her ass off.

"That is so not helping," I hiss over at her.

That just makes her laugh harder.

Bitch.

The twins, having heard the commotion, fly up into the kitchen.

"Mommy, mommy!" they call out in unison. "Is everything okay?"

"Yes, I'm fine, you little dears," Aunt Gertrude tells them. "Just go back and play your video games."

Too late, as one twin notices the boxes and yells out, "Oooh, donuts. Cool, I want one."

"Me too," the other cries out.

The first one reaches over to Benny's special-order box, but his mother swats his hand away.

"Don't touch those. Don't even look at them," she spits out. "Those donuts are *bad.*"

Funny thing is, stuffy Aunt Gertrude, for all her bluster, can't seem to keep her eyes off the donuts in the box.

Brent yells down from the living room, inquiring if everything is all right.

I yell back that everything is fine and we'll be up in a minute.

Sighing, I lean in and take another peek inside the box.

Hell, even I have to laugh. Benny's special-order creations really are hilarious. The donuts I thought were churches are definitely *not.*

I totally thought they were, though, at first when Aunt Gertrude opened the box. One of them was flipped over and the big protrusion up the middle looked just like a steeple, I swear.

But a steeple it was not.

Nope, the "steeple" on each donut is actually a dick. And the "church" part is a set of big balls.

That's right—Benny's special-order donuts are dick and ball-shaped concoctions. And wow are they ever, um, detailed.

I let out a snort when I notice trails of white icing spewing over the tops of some of the "steeples."

"That is so *not* funny," Aunt Gertrude scoffs when she spots the same thing.

Then why are you licking your lips? I think to myself.

"You have to admit that it's a little amusing," I say to her.

"No, it's more like a *lot* amusing," Lainey corrects.

The kids are curious now and trying even harder than before to stand on their tiptoes so they can see what's so interesting inside the box.

Aunt Gertrude puts a stop to that by shooing them away.

"Go find something to do," she admonishes.

They start to leave, looking dejected, but I stop them.

"Wait," I say to their mom, "there are other donuts they could have. Clean ones," I clarify.

I raise a questioning brow at Aunt Gertrude, and surprisingly she nods and says, "Sure, why not?"

Lainey, the new voice of reason, hisses, "Aubrey, wait, hold up. Do you really think those little monsters need freaking *sugar* right now? They're already in a permanently wound-up mode."

"I'm sure one donut won't hurt," I reply.

She shrugs, murmuring, "Whatever you say, Aubrey. It's your funeral."

Ignoring her dramatics, I snip the string off one of the unopened boxes of donuts, and—thank goodness—it's not one of Benny's perverted creations.

As I hand each kid a glazed donut shaped like a rocket, Lainey snickers and says under her breath, "Those could be construed as perverted too, you know? Not only are they totally phallic-shaped, but all that glaze kind of resembles Nolan's face after he's done eating m—"

"*Maple* syrup," I finish for her when I notice Ricky and Ronny are listening in intently.

"Yeah, that stuff is sticky," I go on. "Syrup, that is. It gets all over me too."

Thankfully, the kids lose interest in our conversation and run off with their donuts so that they can return to their video game with Benny.

Though, wait, he's just walked into the kitchen, meaning the kids must've run upstairs or he would've seen them.

"What's going on in here?" Benny asks.

"Umm…"

He sees his donuts and exclaims, "Hey, someone opened my boxes. I saw you'd picked them up, but I was saving those for a surprise later."

"They were a surprise all right," I grumble.

He looks over at Aunt Gertrude and gets it.

"Oh. Ohhh... Jeez, I'm sorry." Benny lowers his head and peers up at her with his best puppy dog apologetic eyes. "I hope you can find it in your heart to forgive me for my indiscretion, ma'am."

I roll my eyes at him.

But it works. Just like that, Aunt Gertrude's whole demeanor changes.

"Oh, no worries," she says to Benny. "I was young once too. Not that I'm old now. Anyway, the point is that I remember doing silly things like that myself."

Really? You had dick-and-balls donuts made? I doubt that.

Of course, I keep all those thoughts to myself.

Aunt Gertrude continues to talk—and blatantly flirt—with Benny.

Lainey and I just gawk at each other, shocked. She must really have it bad for our friend.

That's pretty much confirmed when she picks up a dick donut, one of the ones with the white trail of icing, and bites right into the tip.

"Mmm, dis ith delith-cios," Aunt Gertrude murmurs around

a mouthful of gooey goodness.

"You should try it for real," Lainey cracks under her breath.

I elbow her in the side. "Shut up! She's going to hear you."

Lainey shrugs. "So what if she does? It's true."

"You are so bad."

"You know it, sis."

Benny, working Aunt Gertrude like a puck on a stick, hands her a napkin.

"You have a little bit of icing, um…right about there." He touches the side of his own mouth to show her where she needs to wipe.

"Oh, dear…" She dabs, but at the wrong spot. "Did I get it?" she asks.

"No. Here, let me." Benny takes the napkin from her and wipes away the icing. "There 'ya go," he says once Aunt Gertrude is cleaned up.

She, of course, is still all smiles and blushes.

"Why, thank you, Benjamin. You really are such a kind young man." She reaches out and runs her hand down his beefy, muscular arm, murmuring, "And you're so big and strong too."

Snorting, I say to Benny, "Hey, big strong man, think you can grab this platter and take it upstairs for me?"

He nods, and I hand him the dish, with only "clean" donuts on it.

The "churches" are still in the boxes, which we close…and

tape…and put up high so the twins can't reach them.

Finally, Lainey fixes the coffee, and then we all head back up to the living room, donut crisis averted.

19

HEY, I KNOW THAT GREEN GLOW

BRENT

Aubrey, Lainey, Aunt Gertrude, and Benny all return to the living room.

Whatever problem that was at hand seems to be behind them.

Good, I really didn't want to have to hobble downstairs.

I notice that Benny is carrying a big platter of donuts. And Lainey has the coffee.

Ever the waitress at heart, she begins expertly pouring hot brew into china cups for everyone.

Meanwhile, Benny starts walking around with the donuts, allowing us to choose whichever ones we want.

Aubrey sits down beside me on the sofa where she was before and teasingly asks, "Miss me?"

I reach over and rub her knee. "Always, babe."

Hey, don't laugh. It's true. I enjoy being around her as much as possible.

Good thing I'm marrying her, eh?

"Hey, what took you so long down in the kitchen? And why in the hell was Aunt Gertrude screaming like a banshee?"

She rolls her eyes and assures me, "You don't even want to know."

"Shit, are you kidding? Now I want to know more than ever."

Everyone is chowing down on their donuts and chatting away—guess the caffeine and sugar's already kicking in—so no one's paying much heed to me and Aubrey.

We may as well continue our own private conversation.

Shaking her head, but smiling over at me, Aubrey says, "Let's just say Benny's special-order donuts gave your aunt quite the shock."

Since I can only imagine what he had designed, I let out a chuckle. "Let me guess. He had dirty donuts made?"

"Very dirty donuts," she confirms. "Worse yet, the damn twins showed up to see why their mom was yelling."

I realize then that I've been assuming all this time that, even though Benny is up here with us in the living room, the twins are still downstairs playing video games.

But if they were in the kitchen…

And then they left…

Uh-oh.

"Babe, where are the boys?" I carefully inquire.

Shit, shit, shit, this could be bad.

Aubrey replies, "I don't know. I gave them a couple of donuts and—"

"Great, just what they needed…sugar."

Aubrey snorts, "You sound just like Lainey."

Really?

It's amazing that my soon-to-be sister-in-law was rational for once.

I raise a brow and ask Aubrey, "You don't think they're rambunctious enough?"

"Hmm, good point," she concedes.

I would be content to sit here all night and talk only to Aubrey, but we do have guests.

I'm ready to jump into the general conversation, but suddenly Ricky and Ronny run by, yelling something about playing hide and seek. They continue down the hallway, the one that leads to all the bedrooms.

Guess I know where they are now.

"Hey, you remembered to lock the door to our room, right?" I ask Aubrey.

"Yes," she replies. "I mean, I think I did."

I'm about to get up and check, but then I forget all about the twins when my mom, situated in a chair next to us, leans in and says, "Brent, I can't believe after next Saturday you'll be a married man."

"It is rather shocking that this once wild and crazy guy is finally settling down," Benny, from farther down the sofa, chimes in.

I guffaw. "Ha, you're one to talk. You don't even want us to get into what kind of crap you were once up to."

Benny, blushing, agrees, "No, no, you're right. I don't."

Eliza turns to him and frowns. "Is there more 'crap' you did that I don't know about?"

"No." He gives her a truly loving look. "I've confessed all my former sins to you, my love."

That placates her.

Leaning her head on his shoulder, Eliza says, "You have. And I still love you, because even the bad stuff you did has only made you the wonderful man you are today."

Aunt Gertrude, listening in, gives Eliza the stink-eye.

And Nolan, from over on the love seat next to Lainey, pretends to choke.

"Please, you guys," he says. "No more sweet talk. You're making me ill."

"Me too," Aunt Gertrude mutters.

No one else catches that because Lainey starts gushing over

Nolan.

"Aw, you gorgeous man, stop teasing them. You know you love it when I sweet-talk you like that too. Admit it, you do."

He leans toward her and plants a soft peck on her lips.

"That's only because I've *earned* my sweet talk," he says.

"Mmm, yes, you sure have…"

Lainey begins kissing Nolan, but when she starts crawling into his lap, I clear my throat.

"Hey, we're in mixed company here," I remind them.

Personally, I don't care what they do. I'm used to these two. But I doubt my parents or aunt care to watch Lainey grinding all over Nolan while they make out.

"Oops, sorry." Lainey sits back on the love seat. "I forgot where I was for a minute there."

"Now who's feeling ill?" Benny jokes as he raises his hand.

Nolan shoots him the bird, and even my parents laugh at that one.

But then the entire long hallway off the living room, the one the twins ran down moments ago, lights up in the brightest shade of green.

Fuuuck!

I know that green glow.

Oh yes, I know it all too well.

Aubrey and I turn to each other, horror in our eyes.

Not here. Not now. Not Area 51!

20

ONLY YODA CAN SAVE US NOW

AUBREY

Brent looks at me, aghast, and I, equally horrified, murmur, "Uh, maybe I didn't lock the bedroom door, after all."

"You think?" he deadpans.

He's not happy, but it's too late now. The damage is done.

The monster twins have found the two Area 51 toys I left out on the dresser. I finally located the devices in my luggage and set aside the one I promised Eliza. The other I put right next to it.

"B-b-but they were in packages," I stammer. "How'd the twins get them out?"

Brent snaps, "They're eight, Aubrey, not two. I think they've mastered opening stuff."

I guess they have since, at that exact moment, Ronny and Ricky dance their way into the living room with the Area 51s in hand.

Wonderful.

Now they're in full view of everyone, moving left and right, ducking and advancing, pretending to be sword-fighting…with my freaking sex toys!

"What ever are you doing?" their mother asks.

Thank goodness it's hard to tell what the toys are since they're in motion and glowing bright green.

"We're playing *Star Wars*," one of the twins says.

"Yeah," the other chimes in, "these are our light sabers. We found them in one of the rooms. Aren't they cool?"

Brent may have been horrified at first, but now he's trying not to laugh.

"You're no help," I tell him.

I scan the room, my eyes landing on Nolan.

Hey, he's a go-to kind of guy for fixing bad situations, right? I mean, they don't call him Sensei and Yoda for nothing.

"Do something," I yell over at him.

"What? Why me?" he volleys back.

"Because, well, because you're Yoda," I retort.

"Aubrey," he snorts, enjoying this catastrophe way too much. "Help you, I cannot. On your own, you are."

"You're such an ass," I hiss. "Why do I even try with you?"

"Try, you must," he goes on. "In your nature, it is."

Clearly, Nolan is too busy channeling his inner Yoda to be of any help.

Still, I'm hoping someone will step in before Brent's parents, or Aunt Gertrude, realize what these "light sabers" really are.

Already his dad is cocking his head and murmuring, "What are those things, anyway? They don't look long enough to be light saber toys."

Oh, joy. My soon-to-be father-in-law just has to be a *Star Wars* toy expert.

Ricky—at least I think it's Ricky—beans Ronny over the head with one, and Eliza, who has fully figured out what the green glowing things really are, cries out, "Hey, don't break my Area 51! I haven't even had a chance to try it out yet!"

Both kids stop and, in awe, Ricky asks her, "These cool toys are yours?"

"Yep, they're hers," I reply, throwing my poor friend under the bus.

I'm awful, I know. But I don't want my future in-laws to know what Brent and I do behind closed doors. Imagine them forever envisioning me with a big green glowing fake dick sticking out of my hooha.

No, just no.

"Aubrey!" Brent chastises. "Those aren't Eliza's. They weren't in her room."

I elbow him in the side. "Do you want your mom to know that you use that thing on me? Think of the optics on that one."

That shuts him up.

Yep, now he's just as willing as I to let Eliza fall on the sword. Or on the vibrator, as the case may be.

The twins, though just standing there now, somehow accidentally press something on the Area 51 toys. Suddenly, and with no warning, they start wiggling in their hands, twisting this way and that, because, well, that's what they do.

There's a lot of screaming then when Ricky and Ronny throw the toys at their mom.

Yep, Aunt Gertrude ends up with two squirming, glowing fake dicks in her lap.

"Oh, oh," she huffs. "My, my, whatever do we have here? This house is just all about penises, it seems."

She actually looks intrigued at first, but quickly realizes there's an audience and instantly switches to "mortified" mode.

Lifting the sex toys, one in each hand, she holds them aloft like a victorious queen, and scowls disapprovingly.

There's no doubt about it now—everyone in the freaking room can clearly see exactly what these "toys" really are.

And in the immortal words of Yoda—light sabers, they are not.

21

UH, I CAN EXPLAIN

BRENT

My mom looks at me and rolls her eyes. She knows the sex toys are mine. Pretty much everyone has figured out they're not Eliza's.

And they're all having waaay too much fun with that info.

My dad, well, he can't stop laughing, nor can my teammates quit snickering.

And then there are the girls, chuckling knowingly among themselves.

Everyone's having a good laugh, except for my aunt. She's glaring at me, knowing I'm the one to blame. I guess I have a guilty face.

After she orders the twins to retreat to the downstairs basement, Aunt Gertrude lobs both Area 51s my way, snorting in disgust.

I catch one in each hand and proceed to disengage the glowing *and* wiggling functions.

"Good move," Aubrey whispers as she leans in close.

"Yeah, now if I could only make them disappear."

"Too late," she says. "I think the cat's out of the bag. Or maybe I should say the dick's out of the box."

"Ha-ha, funny girl."

Oh, she's a laugh a minute, this one, especially when she does things like FORGET TO LOCK THE FREAKING BEDROOM DOOR!

I think Aubrey can read my mind, since the words in my head are indeed screaming.

Why else would she peer over at me sheepishly and mutter a heartfelt, "Sorry."

Shit, I can't stay mad at her, though. I just love her far too much.

Softy that I am, I say, "Aw, don't worry about it, babe. I'll take the heat on this one."

And I do.

My aunt begins chastising me. "Brent Oliver, whatever were you thinking, leaving those dreadful things lying around when children were coming over?"

I overhear Lainey gasp, "They're not dreadful. My Area 51 is ahhhh-mazing."

Aunt Gertrude turns her attention to her.

"You have one too?'

"Uh-huh."

"Perverts, all of you, I swear!"

Lainey looks really mad, so before she says something awful to my aunt, I interject, "Hey, in my defense, Ricky and Ronny weren't supposed to raid my bedroom."

Aunt Gertrude pshaws, "Oh, you know how kids are. And if you don't, I'll tell you. They're forever curious. You'll see when you have some of your own one day."

My dad clears his throat. "Now, now, it's not so bad. We're all adults here."

"Ricky and Ronny are *not* adults, Billy," Aunt Gertrude snaps.

My dad levels his sister with a don't-mess-with-me look, and she backs down.

"I meant the people that are currently in this room, Gertrude. *We're* all adults."

She blanches. "Oh, okay. I misunderstood."

My father's not done yet, though.

"Besides," he goes on, "those kids had no idea what those things were. So, as I see it, no harm, no foul. Let's just let it go."

My mom jumps in then. "Actually, we should probably wrap things up and get moving. It is kind of late."

My parents are pros at diffusing tense situations. And they always work in tandem, as a team, like Aubrey and I strive to do.

We're getting better at it. I just hope someday we're as cohesive of a couple as my parents.

I think we will be.

After my parents and aunt gather the twins from downstairs, Aubrey and I walk them to the door to see them off.

We then return to our friends upstairs, only to find Nolan and Lainey have disappeared.

"Hey, where'd my sister run off to?" Aubrey inquires.

Benny snickers. "She and Nolan went to bed. Lainey said she was 'feeling the glow.'"

"I think we all know what that means," Eliza interjects. "Speaking of which…" She nods to the two Area 51 sex toys on the coffee table. "Lainey may have brought her own, but isn't one of those for me?"

Aubrey replies, "Yes, choose whichever one you want. They're both brand new." She hesitates. "Well, maybe not completely unused now that they've been employed as light sabers."

"That's okay," Eliza says. "We'll wash them off. At least we know they're in good working order."

"That we do," Benny says, snickering.

I can tell he can't wait to try out Area 51.

I give him a look and murmur, "Dude."

He knows that means he'll love it.

He tells Eliza to hurry up, so she snatches up an Area 51 from the table and proceeds to check it over.

Turning it this way and that, she muses, "Hmm, so it glows and wiggles, huh? Does it do anything else?"

"It gets brighter as your body warms up," Aubrey says.

Benny scoots over to her so he has a more up-close view. "Babe, we can do so much with this thing," he murmurs.

Okay, all this sex talk, not to mention the fact that Nolan and Lainey are surely getting busy as we speak, has me ready for some action of my own.

"Benny, Eliza." I nod to them both. "Goodnight. Have fun with your new toy."

I grab the other Area 51 that's still on the coffee table and turn to Aubrey. "Come on, babe. Let's say we take a trip to a galaxy far, far away."

22

BRINGING THE GLOW TO MINNESOTA

AUBREY

Brent promises me something otherworldly, and that's exactly what I get.

We don't actually visit a galaxy far away, of course, but it sure feels like we do.

But is it Area 51 providing the magic…or is it Brent?

I believe it's my man.

In fact, I know it's him.

It doesn't matter whether we employ a toy in our fun-times repertoire or not; Brent takes me to places I've never been before. Like right now—he's alternating fucking me with Area 51 and fucking me with his cock.

"Which do you like better, Aubrey?" he rasps as he tosses the glowing green sex toy aside and enters me slowly.

"Unh," I groan, loving every inch he's giving me. "You feel the best, Brent, you. You are always what I prefer."

"Hmm…" He withdraws and thrusts into me forcefully. "That's what I thought."

Peeling up my tee—which we never even bothered to take off, though somehow my bra was lost—he licks my right nipple while his hands slide under my ass so he can lift me up and rhythmically drive into me.

"Ah, I like that," I murmur.

I feel him smiling against my breast, before he moves his mouth up to mine.

Kissing me, he pumps into me so hard and so fast that I'm soon screaming out his name, falling apart.

Brent follows with his own climax, and afterward, in the glow of our lovemaking, we rest in each other's arms.

Wait, wow, it really *is* glowing in here.

Not from us, though.

The whole freaking bedroom is for some reason bathed in lime green.

What the…?

I notice then that the Area 51 toy is lying underneath the window. And it's still on.

Ah, guess it rolled over there when Brent tossed it aside.

Snickering, I remark, "I think we're lighting up the forest all around us right now."

I nod to the toy under the window, and Brent shrugs beneath me. "Eh, I doubt the moose mind all that much."

That makes me laugh.

"Still," I continue, "it's a good thing we don't have any neighbors. They might think a spaceship landed in your backyard."

Brent, chuckling, reaches down and grabs my ass, his fingers trailing seductively to where I'm still so slick and wet.

"Something's about to land," he murmurs as he begins stroking me. "But it's not a spaceship."

That's the end of any further UFO talk.

Later, after Brent is fast asleep, I roll out of bed and finally shut off poor Area 51.

Yeesh, he's looking kind of dim.

Good thing there are plenty of extra batteries in this house.

I go back to bed, but even though I'm tired, I can't seem to find sleep. Tossing and turning, I try everything, even fluffing the pillows up a time or two.

But nothing works.

My body may be exhausted from the day, and even more from the eventful night, but my mind is wide awake.

I hate when that happens.

Sighing, I decide to get back up. Maybe if I sit around out in the living room for a while, sleepiness will find me again.

I'm careful not to wake Brent as I turn down our light, downy comforter and slip out of bed.

After donning a robe to cover my nakedness, I step out into the hall.

Making my way to the living room, I have to pass the other bedrooms. Eliza and Benny's room is dark, there's no light at all coming out from under their door.

But my sister and Nolan's room…

Well, that's a different story.

"Figures," I murmur as I walk on by. "Those two are worse than me and Brent."

I look back.

Yep, there's definitely a familiar green glow blazing out from under their door. I snicker as I think about how we're all bringing the "green glow" to Minnesota tonight.

I'm glad all the people closest to me are so freaking in love… and clearly quite sexually satisfied.

I realize then how truly happy and lucky I am. I'm getting married to the love of my life and life is good, so freaking good.

My inner reflection continues once I'm out in the living room.

But it's really brought home when I slide open the glass doors and step out onto the massive adjoined wooden deck.

"It's so peaceful out here," I murmur to myself, taking it all in—the quiet forest, the cool night breeze.

Brent was right—the moose don't care about any green glow coming from the lake house. It's pure serenity out here.

Leaning against the heavy wooden railing, I peer out into the dark woods. An owl hoots from somewhere off in the distance, and a gentle summer breeze rustles the thick canopy of leaves.

I love the desert out west that we reside in during the hockey season, but there's something so special about the forest. It's mysterious, yes, but it's also a place one can sometimes find answers.

Like I do now, as I realize I've been far too worried about the small stuff, like my lost wedding gown and Brent's sore ankle. So much so that I've been missing the bigger picture.

Brent will be all right. His ankle isn't broken, and based on the latest doctor's report, plus tonight's, er, uh, shall we say performance, he is healing just fine.

As for my dress, it'll arrive eventually. Hell, we have the whole shipping network searching for it at this point.

But even if it doesn't, I'll simply wear another one. What I wear doesn't define my wedding. What matters is that our family and friends are there with us.

Heck, they're already here now.

Well, some of them, though the rest will be in town soon.

What's even more awesome is they're coming to celebrate the love Brent and I have for one another.

Our love is such a beautiful thing.

A sense of peace comes over me then.

And when I go back inside, returning to the bed I share with Brent, I enjoy the best sleep I've had in a long, long time.

23

THINGS TURN AROUND

BRENT

Aubrey tells me the next morning about how last night she went out on the deck and found solace in the forest. As a result, she now has this strong feeling that everything will work out just fine.

I try out my ankle to test her assertion, and wouldn't you know it—I'm able to bear a good deal of weight on it with no discomfort.

"Holy hell," I cry out, happy with this positive development, "maybe you're on to something, babe."

Coming over to me and standing on her tiptoes, she deposits a quick peck on my lightly stubbled cheek.

"Haven't you learned yet that wives are always right about everything?" Aubrey murmurs in my ear.

I step back and raise a brow. "Ah, but you're not my wife quite yet."

"I will be, Brent, in just a little over a week. You may as well get used to married life now."

Laughing, I sit down on the edge of the bed.

"And this is how it's going to be for us once we're married, you always being the one who's right?"

"You know it," she replies smugly. "So get used to it."

In a silly voice, I reply, "Are you saying you're the boss of me now, woman?"

"Mmm-hmm."

More serious, I rasp, "Is that so? We'll just see about that."

Before she knows what's happening, I pull her down to me.

As we fall back together on the bed, her squealing the whole way, I tell her, "I think it's time for *me* to show *you* how it's going to be."

Her panties are down and off in a heartbeat as I flip her over. And then my head is down under that cute little floral sundress she's wearing so fast that Aubrey doesn't know what's happening to her.

"Brent!" she cries out. "Oh damn…"

Touching my tongue to her clit a second time, I murmur, "Who's the boss now?"

"You are," she gasps. "Oh, Brent, you are."

"Good girl."

I grin before I resume what I started. And after another touch of my tongue, this time with a little swirl added in, Aubrey's gasping and begging for more.

She gets more…and so do I.

I conclude that maybe we are each the boss…just at different times.

Yeah, I like that.

Later, I'm thinking that Aubrey really must be a predictor of the future. What she said this morning about everything working out is coming true.

Not just for me and my almost-good-as-new ankle, but wouldn't you know it, around noon that day, we get word that her dress has come in.

Finally!

"And it's okay?" she asks the salesperson on the other end of the phone. "It's not damaged or anything, right?"

I guess the person tells her that it's fine because Aubrey pumps her fist in the air and cries out, "Yes!"

Lainey comes in to see what all the fuss is about.

Once she learns the dress is in, she says to Aubrey, "Let's go pick it up right away, before they lose it again. Besides, we have something we need to do in town, anyway."

Aubrey wraps up with the bridal shop, and turning to Lainey, says, "Sure, we can leave now. But what other thing do we have to do in town?"

I'm a little curious myself so I hang around to find out.

Lainey, smiling ever so slyly—*uh-oh*—says, "Why, we have to go lingerie shopping, sister dear. You have things for your wedding night, sure, but you need some sexy panties and bras for the honeymoon."

"Hmm, good thinking," Aubrey replies.

We're honeymooning at a private resort in the Caribbean. We considered another option, but settled on the Caribbean after that first one fell through. One of my teammates, Noel Sandlund, owns a really sweet beach house on a private island off the coast of Florida. That was option number one since it really would've been an idyllic, romantic location.

But before we had decided, damn Jaxon Holland, another teammate of mine, nabbed the place.

That's okay. Jaxon needs the respite. Poor guy has taken a hell of a lot of heat recently. Much of the blame of our heartbreaking playoff loss fell on him.

Because he's on that private island now, he won't make it up to Minnesota for the wedding.

I talked with him just the other day and he said there'd be way too many flights here and back.

Who is he kidding?

I suspect him not being able to come up here has more to do with the hot girl I hear is down on the island with him than with flight schedules.

That's all right. It's all good. It'd be cool if Jaxon had someone important in his life. He needs the grounding.

But back to where we were—talking lingerie as I recall. Specifically, Aubrey in lingerie, lingerie I can take off her on our honeymoon.

Mmm, yes…

"Babe," I rasp, my voice a little rough from all the racy thoughts running through my head. "I agree with Lainey. You should definitely pick up your dress as soon as possible, and then get in *a lot* of lingerie shopping."

24

LINGERIE FOR THE WIN

AUBREY

On our way out of the house, Lainey and I run into Eliza and Benny. They're coming back from lunch, and when we mention that we're going lingerie shopping after we pick up my dress, the one that's finally come in, Benny insists Eliza should go with us.

She gives him a confused look. "But I thought you wanted to show me nine kinky things we can do with a donut?"

I don't even want to know what that means, but Lainey, of course, does.

"What type of donuts are we talking about here?" she inquires. "Do you mean those dick and ball-shaped ones?"

Benny nods, and Eliza elbows him in the ribs. "Don't tell her that. She might steal the rest and use them with Nolan."

"Hmm, I might," Lainey admits, snickering.

Benny retorts, "Oh, no you won't, because Eliza here is going with you to the lingerie shop. And while you're gone, I'll be hiding my donuts."

"Good," I snort, "'cause I'm not touching any more of those things. God knows where they've been."

Eliza clucks her tongue and rolls her eyes. "Aubrey, we wouldn't put them back in the box after using them."

"Yeah," Benny chimes in. "I'd probably just eat 'em. Can't let a perfectly good donut go to waste, right?"

"Blech..." I make a face. "You are so gross."

"Why do you say that?" Benny wants to know, looking genuinely bewildered. "They're still good. Sure, sometimes the donuts are a little mushy from where they've been and all, but they're, all in all, just fine."

We all gag at that lovely image.

Well, not Eliza.

I swear Benny could say or do anything and she'd think it was cute.

Lainey, snorting, tells Benny, "You take piggishness to a whole new level."

He volleys back, "You're one to talk."

"You guys..." I throw my hands up in the air. "Are we going

lingerie shopping or not?"

Turns out we are.

And Eliza is indeed coming with us.

We head down to the car, while Benny runs off to hide his donuts.

On the way into town, the girls and I talk about the wedding.

Lainey looks over at me and says, "Now don't forget, Aubrey, you need something old and something new."

"Oh, and something borrowed and something blue," Eliza chimes in from the back seat.

"I have something new," I tell them. "The dress that finally came in should count for that."

"What's your 'something old,' then?" Eliza wants to know.

"Her granny panties," Lainey chortles.

I smack her arm off the center console. "I do not own any granny panties, jerk. And for your information, I have a beautiful white silk bra, panty, and garter I plan to wear under my wedding dress. You know that."

"Aw," Eliza coos, "I bet Brent will like that."

"Bet he'll like taking them off even more," Lainey adds.

"So back to our conversation," I say, shaking my head. *These two.* "For the 'something old,' I'm wearing my grandmother's pearl necklace."

"Brent will like that too," Lainey interjects, snickering. "But what he'll really like is when it's off and he can give Aubrey his own version of a pearl necklace."

We're at a red light, and I glare over at her. "You just never stop, do you?"

"What?" she protests. "It's true and you know it."

Ah, hell, it kind of is.

So I let it go.

"What are you borrowing?" Eliza asks.

"Well, the necklace is also borrowed. It belongs to my mom. Lainey, though, is lending me a lace handkerchief for if I have to cry at the ceremony. That'll be my official 'borrowed' item. "

"That's right." Lainey turns to me. "See, Aubrey, not everything I do is perverted."

We reach the bridal shop, and after I park, I remind my sister, "Uh, let's not forget you first wanted to loan me your Area 51."

Eliza coughs. "Ew, gross."

Looking back at her in the rearview mirror, I nod. "I know, right?"

"Hey, I was only kidding about that," Lainey retorts. "You know I'd never loan out my precious green buddy."

"Hmm, that's probably true. Though, if it were blue and not green, I might have tried to convince you."

Lainey's big turquoise eyes widen. "So who's the perv now?"

I stick my tongue out at her.

"Just kidding," I sing-song. "I don't want your slimy used sex toy."

Eliza rolls her eyes and mutters, "Sisters."

I want to tell her that I have the very best one in the world, but she and Lainey are already out of the car.

Sighing, I slip out and follow them up to the bridal shop.

As we enter the store, I take note that Stuffy Sales Lady Who Clearly Needs Dick is nowhere to be found.

Aw, that's kind of a shame. Lainey wrapped a brand-new Area 51 just for her. I was told she and Nolan packed an extra one in case hers malfunctioned.

My sister really, *really* loves her fake alien cock.

"Damn, who are we going to give this Area 51 to now?" Lainey says, pouting.

"We'll think of someone," I assure her. "Just put it back in your purse for now."

Lainey places the gift—wrapped in neon green, our go-to wrapping—back into her bag with a huff. I don't tell her that I have an idea on who the gift should go to. I'm saving that for later.

For now we have a dress to pick up!

To my delight, I try on my gown and it still fits perfectly. Plus, there's no damage even though it was lost in shipping package hell.

Yay! I'm good to go.

Things really have turned around.

As the shop employees are zipping my gown into a garment

bag, I notice Lainey is picking out a frilly blue garter from a box on the counter.

Aw, she's the sweetest.

I know it's for me so I'll have my "something blue."

After we leave the shop, we begin our quest to find a Victoria's Secret or something similar so we can get in some lingerie shopping. But there are no such stores in sight, at least not anywhere on the main drag running through town.

"I guess we'll have to drive over to Minneapolis," I say, tapping the steering wheel in time to a song that's playing softly in the background. "Maybe we should hit up the Mall of America?"

"No, wait." Lainey points to a cross street at the light where we're stopped. I see then that there's a tiny shop about two doors down that looks like what we need.

"I think we just found ourselves a lingerie store, ladies," I say.

I make the turn and pull up to the cute little boutique with a sign that lets us know it's the Don't Get Your Panties in a Bunch Store.

"This is perfect," I say.

When we walk up to the entrance, Lainey remarks, "They come up with the cutest store names in this little town, don't they?"

"Right?" I nod. "I was just thinking that."

After a beat, I add, "I'm so happy I chose for my wedding to be here instead of out in Las Vegas."

"It really is nice here," Eliza remarks. "So quiet and picturesque everywhere you turn. I love that there are forests and lakes everywhere too."

"Yeah, I agree. This really is a perfect locale."

Inside the store, we find there's everything from novelty wear, like edible panties, to La Perla merchandise.

I head over to La Perla land, while Lainey rushes to a rack of panties and bras that are about a hundred shades of blue.

She calls out over her shoulder, "Hey, I think I've finally found lingerie that'll match my dress for the wedding. Look at all these shades of blue."

The wedding colors Brent and I chose are ivory and blue. The bridesmaid dresses are a lovely shade of azure, kind of like how the sky is here every day. Lainey has been determined to find the exact shade for her strapless bra and panties so that they'll match her dress.

No wonder she's excited—she is sure to find what she needs here.

"Look how many there are," she cries as she flips through the racks.

Eliza, though not as anal about a perfect match as Lainey, joins her in the perusal.

I run over quickly to remind them, "Pick out something for Chloe too. She and Dylan are flying in on Monday."

Though Chloe is pregnant, she's only about four months along.

That means she's not so big she can't wear cute undergarments.

With my attendants occupied, I turn my attention back to La Perla.

I really do want to wear super-hot lingerie during our honeymoon. Every day Brent undresses me he should find himself a sexy surprise.

With that in mind, I proceed to pick out twenty hot-as-hell bra and panty sets.

My attendants find what they want, as well.

With everyone happy, we direct our attention to a fun little section of the store labeled "Knock His Socks Off."

"Hmm, let's see what we can find over there," Eliza remarks.

"Maybe they'll have something with donuts on it." I smirk. "I bet Benny would love that."

"No doubt," she says.

"Oh my God, holy crap," Lainey blurts out. She grabs something from a table display and holds it behind her back. "You are so going to want this," she says to Eliza.

"What is it?" Eliza asks. "Show me."

Lainey does and we all burst out laughing.

"You have to buy them," I say to her.

Yep, Lainey found exactly what Eliza needs—donut-themed panties. But the best part is that they're edible.

"Wonder what they taste like," Eliza muses.

"Like donuts, I'm sure," Lainey says.

"Probably," I chime in, "but I'm sure Benny will think they're great no matter what they taste like."

Lainey then turns to me. "Okay, Aubs, now we need to find something fun for you and Brent, and also something for me and Nolan."

Since we're in Minnesota, tried and true hockey country, it doesn't take long to come across the hockey-themed lingerie.

Lainey and I end up choosing the same bra and panty set. The bra has crossed hockey sticks on each cup and the panties have a puck on the front, along with the words *Puck Me.*

"Brent is going to die when he sees these," I say.

"Nolan will too," Lainey replies.

"Your guys will be scoring for sure when you wear that." Eliza snickers.

Yeah, I'm pretty sure she's right.

25

HERE'S TO GETTING LUCKY

BRENT

By Monday, with only five days left till wedding day, more people begin to arrive.

Aubrey's parents come into town, as do Coach Townsend and his wife.

A bunch of my teammates also fly in.

Everyone checks into various hotels, except for Aubrey's parents, who opt to stay at a local bed-and-breakfast just down the road.

I offer the lake house as an option, as I have room for them, but they insist they don't want to intrude on "you young people's fun."

Yeah, I like my new in-laws already. I knew they were chill, like their daughters, but they're even more awesome than I realized.

I feel bad that I can't offer up my home to all my incoming teammates, but it's not *that* big.

Still, I make sure to leave a room free for Dylan and Chloe.

Dylan is a really good friend and a groomsman in the wedding and Chloe is a bridesmaid, so, yeah, no, I couldn't leave those two hanging. They're part of our core group of friends, along with Nolan and Lainey and Benny and Eliza.

And that's the crew that is gathered right now in our big backyard surrounded by forest.

Because of the thick woods, it's usually pretty damn dark out here, but tonight we've illuminated the grounds with blazing tiki torches and a big ole strategically placed bonfire.

Coach Townsend and his wife, and both sets of parents, were in attendance earlier, but they've since departed.

We're down to eight—Aubrey and me, Nolan and Lainey, Eliza and Benny, and Dylan and Chloe.

The girls are kicking back on Adirondack chairs they've pulled close to the fire.

I shake my head. Can you believe they were cold?

Go figure.

"It's summertime, you know," I scoffed when they told me that. "It must be like seventy degrees out even though it's evening."

"Brrr…" Aubrey replied. "That's chilly."

Lainey jumped in. "Yeah, I may have to run in and grab a jacket." She turned toward the house, contemplating. "In fact, I think I'm going to do exactly that."

"Ooh, grab Brent's Wolves hoodie for me," Aubrey called out to her.

Women!

I swear it can be perfect out, like tonight, but if one tiny breeze blows, forget it. It's like an arctic blast to them.

"Good thing we all live out in the desert," I say when I'm back over by the guys at the tree line near the edge of the forest.

Nolan chuckles. "Let me guess. The girls are cold, right?"

"You know it."

He laughs. "I'm not surprised. You should've seen Lainey when we flew up to Toronto for a weekend last March. It snowed *maybe* two inches, but you would've thought we were having a goddamn blizzard with the way Lainey kept shivering and complaining."

"Aubrey's the same way," I say. "And to think those two were born and raised in Pennsylvania. Not exactly a tropical paradise."

"They're just spoiled these days," Nolan says. "In every freaking way."

You can tell with the loving way he says it, though, that he doesn't really mind.

And neither do I.

It's actually kind of cute.

Dylan and Benny chime in that since their women are from Arizona and Nevada respectively, Chloe and Eliza think almost everywhere else in the country is cold.

"Except for maybe the southern states," Dylan clarifies.

I glance over and notice then that both Eliza and Chloe have on big, thick hooded sweatshirts. No wonder they weren't bitching; they're fucking dressed for autumn.

"Eliza thinks it's freezing here," Benny says.

"Chloe does too," Dylan adds. "She brought sweaters and hoodies specifically for this trip."

"I can see that," I murmur, nodding over to their hoodie-clad women.

With a roll of my eyes, I take a sip of the beer I've been nursing. I'm fine with making one or two beers last these days. I used to drink to excess, but haven't in ages, thanks to Aubrey.

She really straightened me out two years ago. And she's kept me on the right path with her unconditional love.

I feel like all of us have that now, which prompts me to hold up my cup and make a toast.

"Hey, here's to finding love," I say.

The guys all razz me at first.

"Dude, are you going soft on us?"

"Brent, where's this coming from? What's in that beer, anyway?"

And my personal favorite, courtesy of Nolan: "I think all this fresh, clean lakeside air has made you high."

"Yeah." I laugh. "Guess I need to get back to arid Las Vegas. No, seriously, you have to admit that we're all pretty lucky."

Nolan and Dylan raise their cups in solidarity, as does Benny, though his contains something nonalcoholic, of course.

In the next ten seconds, all you can hear is a resounding chorus of, "Here, here."

26

A REVELATION

AUBREY

Noticing that our guys are having a grand ole time over at the edge of the forest, I jerk my chin in that direction and murmur to the girls, "I wonder what the boys are talking about over there."

"Probably sex," Lainey replies.

I snort. "No, that's your purview. You're obsessed, I swear."

"Like you're not?" She gives me a bitch-please look. "Ms. I-Pass-Out-Area-51s-to-all-my-Friends."

"Hey!"

"I'm surprised you haven't given one to Mom yet."

"That's disgusting, Lainey."

She rolls her eyes. "They have sex, Aubrey. How do you think we got here?"

"I *don't* think about it," I volley back. "And if you keep this up, I'm totally taking away your Area 51, you brat."

"Pfft, over my dead body."

"Mmm," Chloe says, joining in. "That thing is worth a fight to the death over. Dylan and I like our Area 51 so much that we brought it along with us."

"No way! Nolan and I brought ours too," Lainey exclaims.

Chloe and Lainey fist-bump, and Eliza asks, "You brought it even though you're pregnant, Chloe?"

Chloe turns to her. "I brought it *because* I'm pregnant. I swear I'm hornier now than I was before. Besides, how do you think I got knocked up in the first place? After Aubrey gifted me one of those damn things, Dylan and I used it almost constantly. And, well"—she gestures to her baby bump—"that led to *other* things, and here we are."

"I was just kidding," Eliza says. "I was actually the same way. I wanted sex all the time too when I was pregnant. But sadly, there was no one around at the time. I only wish I'd had an Area 51 back then."

"Or a Benny," Lainey says.

"For real," Eliza sighs.

Eliza's baby daddy is Drew Chidders, who's on the Wolves roster. Well, for now he is. There are rumors he may be traded soon.

I kind of hope he is. Drew's in Ava's life now, but he was absent for a very long time.

Plus, he's kind of a jerk.

"Area 51 would've been better even if Drew had been around," I remark.

Eliza chuckles. "You're right about that, Aubrey. But really, I wish I'd known Benny at the time. Not just for sex, he just would've been so sweet and helpful."

Chloe nudges her arm. "Guess you'll have to have one with him and find out."

"Hmm," Eliza mutters slyly. "I guess I will."

I've noticed that Eliza's not drinking tonight, and though I know for a fact she's not pregnant right now—she asked me earlier if I had extra tampons since she'd forgotten to pack some—I can't help but wonder if she and Benny are planning on trying soon.

I suppose we'll find out in a couple more months.

That'd be cool—Chloe with a baby and Eliza pregnant.

That'd leave me and Lainey, out of our whole close-knit group, as the only ones without kids.

Hmm…

I know Lainey and Nolan want to wait a little longer before they start a family, but Brent and I have talked about it and we want to start our family sooner rather than later.

That makes me think—why not start now?

BABY FEVER

BRENT

After the outdoor bonfire gathering ends, Aubrey and I go up to our bedroom. I can tell she has something on her mind. Why else would she be sitting cross-legged on our bed, chewing her lip?

I'm wearing only my boxer briefs and nothing else as I take a seat next to her.

"Okay, Aubs, I know that look. You have something you want to talk about, right?"

"I do," she says quietly. Reaching out and touching my arm, she murmurs, "But first, can I ask you something?"

"Sure, sweetheart."

"Do you love me, Brent?"

"Hey, hey…" I scoot a little closer to her. "Where's this coming from?"

She shrugs and I take her in my arms. I know she feels safest there, and I think she needs a little reassuring right now.

"Aubrey," I say softly, "I love you. In fact, I love you so much that I'm marrying you, babe."

"Yes, yes, I know." She sighs and sits back, but our hands remain joined. "But do you love me enough to have a baby with me?"

Is she kidding?

"Are you kidding?" I reply, echoing my thoughts. "We've already discussed this. You know I can't wait to have children with you."

We *have* talked about this before, so I'm not sure why this is coming up.

But then she murmurs, "When?" and I think I know what's up.

"Babe…" I let go of her hands so I can reach up and cup her beautiful face. "I'm ready whenever you are."

Biting her lip, she quietly asks, "Would you want to start trying now?"

"What? You mean like tonight?"

She nods.

"But aren't you still on the pill?"

Sighing, she says, "I'm supposed to start a new cycle today. But I haven't taken one yet."

Excited now, I blurt out, "Well, hell, I know it can't happen right away, but let's go throw them out—today's pill, tomorrow's pill, and all the rest."

She starts smiling like crazy. "Are you sure?"

"Yes, yes."

Damn, I can't wait for her to ditch those things. I want Aubrey swollen with my baby as soon as possible. And in return I want to be there for her through everything. We can raise our child with all the love and caring we feel for one another.

And hopefully there will be more than just one. That's right—I want a really big family.

In the en suite bathroom, Aubrey removes her fresh pack of pills from her cosmetics bag.

"Well," she says, holding them aloft, "here they are. Do you want to do the ditching honors or shall I?"

"Babe, let's do this the way we do everything."

"And how's that, Brent?"

I grasp the side of the pill packet and say, "Together."

And that, my friends, is how we check off step one of making a baby.

28

STEP TWO

AUBREY

Brent tells me in the bathroom about the steps he's coming up with for making a baby.

"I didn't know it was that long of a list," I remark, laughing. "I think the basics are pretty simple."

"True, but I still like the idea of having a plan," he says.

"A plan, huh?"

"You know it."

Brent is pretty intense once he gets into something. That's why he ended up so good at hockey. He was obsessed with the sport from an early age.

After he and I finish ditching my pills, I ask him what step number two is.

"Oh, now comes the fun part, Aubs."

He waggles his eyebrows, and, for fun, I feign innocence.

"Does this mean it's time for sex?"

Laughing, he grabs me up in his arms and carries me back into our bedroom. I'm thrilled. Not just because I'm about to get it on with a hot hockey player, but the fact that he can carry me with ease is a testament to how well his ankle has healed.

"You bet your ass it's time for sex," he says lustily, finally answering my question as we tumble together onto the bed.

I laugh and cheer, "Yay!"

Brent makes short work of my shorts and the black and red Wolves sweatshirt I put on outside. Since he has on nothing but boxer briefs, those pesky things are off and on the floor in no time.

"Mmm…" I run my hand over his smooth chest and hard abs. "I like you naked, Brent."

"Not as much as I like you naked," he replies huskily, his hands roaming.

With *every* part of him now pressed to me, I murmur, "Hmm, I can tell."

I love this man, and I love how he loves me, which is what he starts doing now.

"Brent," I moan, moving beneath him.

There's no way we can make a baby tonight, not with just

one pill missed. But it's still intense and meaningful, like we're practicing for the real event and putting our all into it.

It will happen too. I know it. I have a feeling I'll get pregnant fast.

Destiny holds it in the cards that Brent and I are meant to have a family. Ever since the day I first met him, in this very bed, it's been meant to happen.

It's funny, though, how I couldn't stand him at first. But I couldn't. I thought he was the biggest jerk.

And here I am now—wanting to have his kids.

How our lives have come full circle.

I realize then that I want to have *lots* of babies with Brent.

So, after we're done loving one another, as we're lying in each other's arms, I bring this up to him.

"How many kids do you want, Brent?"

He tightens his arms around me. "It's really up to you, Aubs. You're the one who has to carry each one around for nine months. And, of course, you have to give birth."

"True, but the idea of that has never bothered me. So, really, I'd be more than okay with having a few."

"A few?" Brent's voice is tentative, but also, I can tell, hopeful. "How many would you consider 'a few' to be?"

"I don't know exactly," I admit. "More than three, I think."

Brent's quiet, so I place my chin on his chest and peer up at him. In the moonlit room, I can tell I wasn't wrong in reading him.

"You want a big family too, don't you?"

Hope swells in my heart.

He nods, a little misty-eyed himself. "Yeah, Aubrey, I kind of do."

"Well, that's good."

I begin trailing tiny kisses on his chest, then down over his abs.

But then I stop for a sec so I can look up at him.

"I'm glad we're in agreement," I say. "But I think that means we definitely need more practice."

Brent chuckles.

He knows where I'm going with this, especially when I take him in my hand and start stroking.

"Babe," he tells me, arching up. "I couldn't agree more."

THE BIG DAY

BRENT

It's finally here.

The day I've been waiting for, the day I was fucking born for, the day that I marry the woman of my dreams—my wedding day.

I wake up in the tiny spare bedroom off from the kitchen and dining room area. It's a room I usually reserve for kids when they stay over, like Ricky and Ronny. I have it decorated in a toy train motif, kind of like Thomas the Train threw up in here.

Man, I feel like I'm four.

Damn Lainey insisted I sleep my last night as a single man separated from Aubrey.

"Why?" I asked her.

"What do you mean why? You can't see your bride the morning of the wedding," she stated adamantly. "That would not be right."

"Lainey," I scoffed, "suddenly the traditionalist. Wonders never cease."

Nolan walked by just then—we were in the upstairs hallway—and as he grabbed her ass, he said, "That's what I keep telling this woman every day of her life. Her ass is a true wonder, for sure."

She swatted his hand away, albeit with a smile.

I just rolled my eyes at them.

"You crazy kids," I teased. "What am I going to do with you?"

"I don't know." Nolan shrugged. "Maybe send us to our room."

He winked at Lainey, and I told the two of them to just go have sex, for fuck's sake.

They did, leaving me standing in the hall.

Thinking about it now, I'm happy for them. It's cool as shit that Nolan, in a few short hours, will be my brother-in-law. Hell, we've been such close friends for so long that he already feels like family.

We may as well make it official.

Speaking of which, the wedding is happening in a few short hours. That means I better get my ass in gear and start moving. There's a lot to do. The church ceremony is at one o'clock, and afterward there are pictures to be taken and a big catered reception back here at the house.

After I get out of bed, I adjust my dick in my boxers and open the door.

"Ack, Mr. Oliver!" A young girl of about nineteen jumps back. "I'm so sorry."

Shit!

The caterers must already be setting up, seeing as the girl is holding a large plastic-covered platter of what looks like cocktail shrimp.

"No worries," I tell her. Motioning to the food, I ask, "Do you need any help with that?"

I kind of forget that I'm in nothing but boxer briefs until she glances down and, biting her lip, murmurs, "Wow…uh… I mean, no. I'm good."

And with that, she scampers off, leaving me chuckling.

I'm not at my nine-point-one inches like when I'm hard, but even "at ease" my guy's still pretty fucking impressive.

Nonetheless, I shouldn't give out any more free shows of the goods to the catering staff. I head back into the bedroom where I can pull on a pair of jeans.

As I'm tugging vintage Levi's up my legs, a slip of paper falls from one of the back pockets.

I reach for it and pick it up off the floor.

When I flip it over, I discover it's not a piece of paper at all. No, it's a strip of photos from a photo booth.

They're pics of me and Aubrey.

"I remember that day," I murmur as I take a seat on the edge of the bed and rake my fingers through my messy hair.

I realize then that I haven't worn these jeans since last October. That's why they were still in this room. At the time, I'd kicked them off downstairs with the intention of taking them down to the laundry room.

But I was too lazy and ended up tossing the damn things into this seldom-used bedroom.

I also recall *why* I was too lazy that day—Aubrey was waiting for me upstairs and I couldn't wait to go to her.

We'd had such an amazing time that beautiful fall afternoon. We'd flown in for a quick weekend getaway when I'd had a couple days off with no games.

It was gorgeous here at the time. Cool, crisp fall days, with all the leaves changing to beautiful colors.

There'd been a fall festival in town that weekend, which we'd gone to on day one.

That's where we took these pictures.

I look down at the strip of photos now.

There's one of Aubs feeding me a caramel apple.

And then one where she's shoving it in my face, and I'm laughing my ass off.

The next one is of us looking at each other, all loving-like.

And finally, in the last pic, the one at the bottom, we're kissing.

What hits me hardest, though, is the tiny tagline in the border.

It reads: *Memories in a Minute that Last for a Lifetime*

Yes!

That's what these pics are—snippets in time of a beautiful fall day spent with the love of my life.

These photos will last a lifetime, just like us.

You know, I bought Aubrey this stunning multi-carat diamond tennis bracelet as my wedding gift to her. But I think I'll wrap this strip of photos up and give it to her, as well.

Crazy as it sounds I have a feeling she's going to love these four simple pics way more than a whole string of diamonds.

And that's because the photos are of love and happiness, which is what we're all about.

30

MARRIED, AT LAST

AUBREY

My wedding is absolute perfection. I couldn't ask for a more perfect day.

It's a whirlwind filled with love and images that I look back on fondly as time moves on.

That's what I'm doing today, reminiscing on a lazy afternoon. Brent and I are back in Las Vegas as he's readying for the new hockey season.

It may be autumn, but I'm still thinking of that beautiful June day, the day I married Brent Oliver.

And this is what I remember…

Getting ready in the morning with the girls and laughing so hard that we ended up crying. I needed that lacy handkerchief from Lainey right there and then, my "something borrowed."

I had already swapped out one white garter for the blue one Lainey bought at the lingerie shop as my "something blue."

There was more than fun and tradition that day too.

There was…

My father walking me down the aisle, both of us sniffling as he gave me away to Brent.

The look of love in Brent's eyes as the minister had us say our handwritten vows, the ones we wrote that Sunday morning.

Brent slipping the ring on my finger, making us official…

Or maybe it was the kiss afterward that really sealed the deal for me.

It was certainly memorable.

And then there were our friends and family cheering us as we were pronounced "husband and wife."

The pictures taken afterward and the random squirrel that photobombed one of the outdoor shots.

And the reception back at the house.

More snippets and images…

Our first dance as husband and wife.

The "naughty" toast Nolan, Brent's best man, gave.

Catching Nolan and Lainey in a spare bathroom later that night, doing the "naughty" things he had talked about during the toast.

Oh, and one of my favorites—*when I pulled Aunt Gertrude aside and gave her the neon-green wrapped Area 51, that extra one from Lainey that we'd taken to the bridal shop.*

I thought she might slap me, but she hugged me instead, thanking me profusely.

Ah, the love I receive for helping people get off.

More memories…

Eliza and Benny leading "The Locomotion" dance train at the reception.

Dylan and Chloe singing along to all the eighties and nineties songs that were played.

What was up with that, by the way?

I don't know.

But what I do know is that the day I married Brent Oliver has gone down as one of the best days in my life.

Only topped by what came next…

EPILOGUE

AN EVERLASTING LOVE ON ICE

BRENT

Ten Years Later...

The years have passed, and I love Aubrey more than ever.

We have a good life too.

No, wait, we have the *best* life.

Not only am I still playing for the Las Vegas Wolves, but we've continued to win more championships. I've accumulated so many trophies and awards for playing top-level hockey that it's not even funny.

More importantly, though, I have the family I always dreamed of.

Aubrey and I have four kids now, two boys and two girls, with another son on the way.

Will we stop now?

Hmm, I don't know.

We're both still young, only in our mid-thirties. And pregnancy is easy for Aubs. She tells me that she's up for more.

She also says that having my babies are the only memories that top our wedding day from all those years ago.

Hmm, so, on the more children thing…

I think we'll just let fate decide.

That's how we've lived our lives so far, so it makes the most sense.

Destiny brought us together.

Well, hockey and destiny.

I met Aubrey when she became my life coach. So the two are forever entwined in my mind.

I like to tell people that we went from "destiny on ice" to "vows on ice."

But really there's one more—our ongoing story is an "everlasting love on ice."

And that, my friends, is the very best "on ice" of all.

THE END

What's up next for the Boys of Winter hockey rom-com series?

Noel's story, ILLUSION ON ICE, releases this winter!

But before that comes out, there's a football romance spin-off series on the way.

That's right, due to popular demand, Graham Tettersaw, Chloe's brother, will have his own story coming out this fall. The title is *Forward Progress* (Men of Fall #1).

Follow me on Amazon to be notified of these new releases.

ABOUT THE AUTHOR

S.R. Grey is an Amazon Top 30 and a #1 Barnes & Noble bestselling author. Her newest bestselling hockey rom-com series features a different hot player in every story. Plus, they can be read in any order since they're all interconnected standalones.

Ms. Grey's novels have appeared on multiple Amazon bestseller lists, including the Top 100 several times. She is also a Top 100 bestselling author on iTunes.

Author Website (stop on by to see how pretty it is):
http://srgrey.com/

S.R. Grey's Facebook page is a hoot:
http://www.facebook.com/SRGrey

S.R. Grey's Facebook Reading Group is even MORE fun:
https://www.facebook.com/groups/
SRGreyHardAbsandHotBooks/

Sign up for S.R. Grey's newsletter (you know you want to):
http://mad.ly/signups/106801/join

S.R. Grey on Twitter (for the random tweets):

https://twitter.com/AuthorSRGrey

S.R. Grey on Instagram for the riveting pics (well, she thinks so):

http://instagram.com/authorsrgrey

S.R. Grey Goodreads Author page:

http://www.goodreads.com/author/show/6433082.S_R_Grey

ACKNOWLEDGEMENTS

Thank you to the readers, bloggers, ARC team members, and *everyone* who loves and supports this fun series. You're all amazing and I appreciate each and every one of you.

Thank you, Kristin S., Barbara H., Franci N., and Julie D. for shining up *Vows on Ice*.

And thank you to Heidi P. for providing the Minnesota "inspiration."

Lastly, a huge shout out to my family, friends, and esteemed hockey "consultants."

Y'all make this beautiful journey possible.

Wait!

It's not over yet.

Here's the first chapter of DESTINY ON ICE, the story of how Brent and Aubrey met and fell in love. It's also the first novel in the bestselling *Boys of Winter* series.

1

GOLDEN BOY GETS A LITTLE TARNISHED

BRENT

My father was a great hockey player. Back in the day, in the era of eighties' big hair and synthesized music, Billy Oliver won not just one, but two Stanley Cups. He was awarded the Conn Smythe trophy both times and has received an assortment of other hardware throughout the years.

He's retired now, but my dad was once a star.

To me, though, he's always just been Dad.

But as his only child, I have a legacy to live up to. I pray I don't disappoint him. I pray someday I'll be as good as he once was. And damn it, I better win a freaking Stanley Cup like he did.

I have no choice, not really. Since the moment my father first laced up hockey skates on my three-year-old little feet, the look of pride on his face told me even then all I needed to know—anything short of being the best will never do.

And guess what?

In many ways, I've become the best at what I do, which is, like my dad, play professional hockey.

I've been good since the start, a natural some say. I don't know about that, but I do know that even before I was drafted—in the first round by the Las Vegas Wolves, an expansion team at the time—I was being called "The Golden Boy" and "The Next One."

These days, three years later, I'm pretty much the poster boy for the NHL. And I have a slew of endorsement deals to prove it.

Lately, though, I've been falling short.

And I really don't know why.

Something is missing for me in the game. Or is it something that's missing in *me*?

I blow out a breath and shake my head.

Things started out so great. Where'd it all go wrong?

I made a name for myself early on. Expansion teams usually struggle for years before posting a winning record. Not so for the Wolves. With me centering what was then a subpar line, I was still able to make us shine. We came out swinging that first season in the league.

BRENT OLIVER SCORES THE GAME-WINNING GOAL IN HIS AND THE WOLVES' FIRST NHL GAME, SETS UP TEAMMATES FOR TWO MORE

One month later, there was this:

THE WOLVES OFF TO A COMPLETELY UNEXPECTED STELLAR START

Then things started to slide.

Those subpar players on my line weren't enough to keep afloat a pretty much overall crappy team, even with me centering. The Wolves' owners and management made the necessary moves— they don't mess around when shit needs to get done.

We picked up a phenomenal winger, Nolan Solvenson. He started to play and things turned around.

ADDING SKILLED RIGHT-WINGER NOLAN SOLVENSON TO ROOKIE BRENT OLIVER'S FIRST LINE PROVING TO BE A MASTERFUL MOVE

ON A MID-SEASON WINNING STREAK, THAT SOLVENSON TRADE IS PAYING OFF FOR THE WOLVES!

Another trade made at the deadline gave us Benjamin Perry. A big, strong left-handed winger, he was the final piece to the puzzle. Even with far-from-elite second, third, and fourth lines, it didn't matter. Not with me, Benjamin, and Nolan on the first line. We could *not* be stopped.

Benjamin—or Benny, as he's known to the team—is adept at using his size and muscle to check the hell out of any sorry soul who happens to be matched up against him. He simply wears other players down…and then it's a fucking scorefest. Thanks, in part, to his killer slapshot.

Together with Nolan, a sniper in his own right, we were—and in many ways still are—quite a force to be reckoned with. We destroy teams, though not as much lately. But back then, man, we were racking up so many points that the press branded us the OPS line, as in Special Forces.

THE OPS LINE'S SNIPERS OF OLIVER, PERRY, AND SOLVENSON ELIMINATE THE COMPETITION WITH EASE

THERE'S NOTHING COVERT ABOUT THIS LINE'S SCORING PROWESS

We worked our reputation to our advantage. Trash-talking on the ice and taunting players became our pastimes. We also happened to get a lot of pucks in the net.

Ah, the good old days.

We still trash-talk and taunt, but we aren't as lethal as we once were.

"We just need to get back on track," I murmur to myself. "The season doesn't start for a few more weeks. I'll have my shit together by then."

I better, since I'm the captain of the team. If I go down, we all sink. And that's not fair to anyone, especially not to my linemates, Nolan and Benny. Over the past couple of years they've become my best friends, which is a blessing and a curse. It's a blessing that we play so well together, but it's a curse that we also have a tendency to fuel each other's vices.

God knows this off-season we've become far too focused on partying and women. Like me, my linemates are extremely popular. Hell, let's not mince words—we're gods. In the hockey world, it's good to be a god. Guys want to *be* you and girls want to *do* you. Multiply that all by a hundred if you're not an ogre in the looks department.

And none of us are.

Not to brag—though, I guess I kind of am—but I have the most women falling at my feet. Hell, I've had women who've wanted to *lick* my feet.

Like, literally.

There was this crazy bitch this one time…

Wait, I digress. Back to where our team is today—floundering in a sea of mediocrity.

After that first good regular season, we fell apart during the playoffs. A dirty hit that sent me flying into the boards also sidelined me with a concussion. It didn't end there. More bad luck plagued our team. Nolan went into a scoring slump, and Benny took a punishing check against the boards that broke his foot. We were knocked out of the playoffs in the first round.

I went to Minneapolis, my hometown, to sulk.

"Next year will be different," my always-positive father tried to reassure me.

He was wrong.

We missed the playoffs entirely the following year, for reasons still unknown.

Then there was the season that just ended this past spring—another disappointment.

LAS VEGAS WOLVES FOLD, KNOCKED OUT ONCE AGAIN IN THE FIRST ROUND

Needing a break from all things desert-life, I said to Nolan and Benny, "Fuck this shit."

That was over three months ago. We were in the middle of cleaning out our lockers for the summer. My linemates looked at me, confused.

And then Nolan finally asked, "Fuck what shit, Oliver? What are you going on about over there?"

"Everything," I replied, gesturing around the empty locker room. "We're done, finished. Let's get the hell out of this place for a while."

I meant Las Vegas the city—and I think Nolan was catching my drift—but Benny misunderstood.

"Dude," Benny began, "we *better* get outta here soon." He checked his watch. "We have a tee time at two."

He meant the golf game we had planned, but I was having none of that.

"Fuck golfing," I snapped. "I'm talking about *really* getting out of here. I think we deserve a much-needed break from this whole damn town."

Nolan looked intrigued. "What'd you have in mind?"

I happily shared with him and Benny what I'd been thinking about for days. "Let's head up to my house in Minnesota. We can spend the summer on the lake." I grinned, bad intentions in mind. "You know I'm a fucking rock star up there. We can party every night. Hell, we can fuck and get fucked up till training camp starts up in September."

Benny was in immediately, but Nolan had to think it over in his thoughtful kind of way.

At last, he said, "Okay, let's do it."

Since that day we've been partying like rock stars. Or, more accurately, like out-of-control hockey players.

We're still on a roll, even though it's August and we have to fly back to Vegas real soon. Until then, however, I've vowed my cool contemporary house by the lake will remain *the* place to party. It's our OPS base for debauchery, after all.

In reality, though, this craziness can't go on. We all know that.

Even wild and crazy Benny had the sense to ask me just last week, "Dude, what should we do?"

"About what?"

I was in the midst of texting a local puck bunny to see if she wanted to meet me for a quickie, so I was a bit distracted.

Benny sighed. "We gotta report to camp in a less than a month. Guess it's time to start thinking about slowing down with the girls, the booze, the—"

I put down my phone and cut him off with a raucous, "Hell no, my friend. We just need to scale it back a little."

"Scale it back in what way?" Nolan, who walked in the room just at that moment, wanted to know.

I shrugged. "Maybe have smaller parties? Maybe drink a little less?"

We all agreed to those things, but we haven't followed through. In the past seven days we've abstained from partying for all of two.

This is so not going to play well with the team. My diet is crap, and I'm nowhere near peak playing shape. Sure, my body looks all lean and cut, meaning you'd never know I wasn't ready to hit the ice rearing to go, but looks can be deceiving. I went out for a run just the other day and came back fucking winded as hell.

That was a first.

Still, I'm confident I can get back into playing shape in no time. It's the inside of my head that's kind of a mess. I just don't fucking care about winning, not anymore. I mean, I do, but I don't. Does that make sense?

Nah, it doesn't to me, either. But I better figure it out, and fast.

Where's my drive to get my shit together? Where's my commitment to winning, my obligation to my players?

I ask myself these things every day now, but I guess the answers are clouded by my drinking copious amounts of alcohol and fucking way too many puck bunnies.

Dad would be so proud—not.

Well, he would be glad I diligently use protection. I haven't gone *that* far off the rails. Still, wrapping my dick up isn't enough to keep management off my ass. My agent already informed me—this morning, in fact—that the Wolves' ownership group has a pretty good idea of what I've been up to, along with my teammates, here in Minneapolis.

I listened half-heartedly when my agent woke me up to say, "Don't blow this off, Brent. Management is *not* happy with you. There's a certain image they expect you to uphold, and you're not doing that."

God forbid I'm not the team's "Golden Boy." I'm "The Next One," remember?

Bullshit, it's all crap.

Coach Townsend called me shortly after I got off the phone with my agent. He had the same warning.

"You don't want the team to take action. You're not going to like what they have in store for you, Brent, if you keep up with this bad behavior."

"Oh, come on," I replied, laughing. "The Wolves can't fire me. And what could be worse than that?"

Coach T chuckled like he knew something.

Hmm…

"I can't worry about that shit today," I said to him. "I'll start cleaning up my act tomorrow."

"Brent…" Coach T sounded doubtful.

"Really, I will," I insisted.

That was a few hours ago. And I plan to make some changes. But maybe not quite yet.

"Before tomorrow gets here," I justify to myself, "we still have the rest of today. And that means there's time for one more party."

I stride into the second-floor living room of my house, a spacious and angled space overlooking the huge lake on my property. Peering out at the crystal blue water, I announce to Benny and Nolan, "Listen up, boys. We're having one final blowout tonight, a party to end all parties."

There's a murmur from Nolan, but nothing from Benny.

"We're going to do this one right," I go on. "We party tonight. But then, when tomorrow arrives, we're done with messing around. We start training full-on."

Yeah, right, a little voice in my head coughs out.

I look around since no one besides my guilty conscience seems to be chiming in.

It's early afternoon and the sun is bathing the room—my favorite, by the way, with the way it juts out over the lake showcasing the floor-to-ceiling windows on two sides and a massive deck with a mile-long view on the other—in a warm summer glow.

Nolan, who is lounging on an easy chair with a beer in his hand, raises his bottle. "I'm in," he says.

His words aren't the least bit slurred, even though he's been drinking straight through since last night's bash.

"And then, yeah," he continues, agreeing with me, "we'll start getting ready for camp."

Despite his ability to suck down alcohol like a fish, Nolan hasn't veered too far off course. Getting back on track won't be hard for him. He's like Mr. Discipline. And he's not fooling anyone, anyway. I caught him working out in my basement gym a few days ago. With the way he was pumping iron I suspect he's been training consistently for a few weeks now.

There's still not been a response from Benny, which is unusual. Dude's always up for a party. He's probably the worst of us when it comes to out-of-control antics.

And that's saying a lot.

"Hey, where's Benny?" I ask Nolan as I scan the shadows of the room.

He nods to a sofa that's been pushed way-ass off to a far corner.

"Oh, I should've known." I chuckle as I take in an eyeful.

Benny is sprawled out on a sofa in the shadows, sleeping like a baby. His massive chest is rising and falling in perfect rhythm with the ticking clock on the stone mantel above his head. Some puck bunny he was fucking around with last night is with him, passed out on top of him.

The sheet covering their naked bodies is hiked up just enough to afford a view of the girl's creamy thigh, which is casually slung over my linemate's muscular, hairy-as-hell leg, and positioned under his semi-exposed junk.

Chuckling at Benny's total lack of modesty, I pick up a throw pillow and lob it at his head—the one that clearly controls all his thinking.

And he scores!

As the pillow makes contact—and how could it not with a pole like that marking my target?—the sheet falls off completely. I get a quick flash of perky tits and tiny ass. And then, shit—a big honking piece of man-meat assaults my eyes.

"Dude," I snort, mock-offended. "You need to cover that shit before you blind us all."

Benny stirs to life. Sitting up, he barks, "What the fuck, Oliver? I was having the best dream ever. That is till you started tossing shit at my balls. "

Nolan lets out a low chuckle. "Only you, Benny, could find a way of using 'tossing' and 'balls' in the same sentence. But really"—he tilts his bottle to Benny's dick—"you need to do what Brent said and cover that shit up."

Throughout this entire brain-draining exchange, the girl wakes up. And damn, she looks young. Letting out a little squeak, not unlike a hamster, she gathers the sheet around her naked self and scurries off to where she seems to think the bathroom is.

I only know this 'cause she's muttering something about having to pee. But the poor girl has no idea where to go. Hamster-girl flies past me, heading down the wrong hallway, the one that leads to my bedroom.

As I rush to retrieve her, I can't help but grumble, "Why in the hell do they always think the damn bathroom's down *my* hall?"

I catch up to and redirect the girl, pointing her in the correct direction. "It's that way, sweetheart," I say in my kindest tone.

No need to be an asshole; the poor thing already looks shell-shocked. Though whether that's due to waking up in a strange house or waking up next to that monstrous thing Benny calls a cock, I have no clue.

"Thanks, Mr. Oliver," she replies.

And then she runs off.

"*Mr.* Oliver?" I shake my head. "What the fuck is up with that? If she thinks I'm old and I'm only twenty-two, then..."

Whoa, wait.

Hurrying back out to the living room and pointing an accusatory finger at Benny, I say, "That chick better be over eighteen, dude. We're in enough trouble already with the team."

Benjamin Perry is twenty-eight, but he likes younger girls. Nothing illegal, so don't get your panties in a bunch. He just happens to favor babes who either look young, or are *just* old enough.

"She's twenty-three," he replies, sounding hurt by my accusation.

"What? Five years past eighteen?" Nolan peers over at me and smirks. "Hey, Oliver, you think Benny is working up to go cougar on us?"

Laughing, I reply, "Seeing as he's on his way to fucking the full spectrum of girls in their twenties, I do indeed think he's secretly working his way up to thirty."

"Small steps," Nolan says.

"Fuck you," Benny interjects. "You're both dickheads."

I put up my hands. "Hey, don't be pissed at me. Take it up with Nolan. He started with the jokes. I only brought up the chick's age for your own protection. I'm always looking out for you, buddy."

"Yeah, you usually are," he concedes. "And thanks for that." He shoots me an apologetic grin. "You really are a good kid at heart."

I shrug, feeling a little self-conscious at being called a kid. But then I see what Benny is up to, preparing to bust my balls.

Sure enough, the next words out of his mouth are "You

do know I mean *kid* in a good kind of way. Like maybe"—he smirks—"a *golden boy* sort of style."

"Ha. Ha," I retort. And since he's enjoying yanking my chain far too much, I shoot him the bird. "Shut the fuck up, man."

Benny may give me a hard time, but his underlying sentiment is genuine. What he said about me being a good guy, like a decent person, is true. Despite all the craziness of late, I want nothing but the best for my friends. And just because I've been fucking up my own life lately doesn't mean Benny's and Nolan's lives have to go down the shitter too.

Really, I probably should've never invited them to Minnesota. I should have come up to the lake house by myself. That would've been the smart thing to do, especially if my intention all along has been to piss away my career.

I don't really want that, though, do I?

No.

I just need some help in getting back on track.

But where would I find something like that?

Ah, fuck it.

"So what do you say, Benny?" I ask, back to focusing on the party. "You in?"

He stretches, covering his dick with the pillow I threw at him. I make a mental note to have all my furniture *and* their decorative accents, especially the pillows, steam cleaned.

Running his hand through his shaggy, dark blond hair, he

says, "Am I in for what?"

"Party tonight," Nolan interjects in his usual no-nonsense tone. "One last blowout, and then Brent here says we're stopping with the bad behavior."

I have to laugh. Nolan is only three years older than me, but it's like he's twenty-five going on forty. He's the voice of reason in our crew.

Well, most of the time.

Not today, though. No, today he agrees to go all-out.

With the party plans full steam ahead, we get on our phones, texting and calling everyone we know.

"Tonight we party hard," I declare when we reconvene in the living room.

"Yeah," Nolan says, holding up a freshly opened bottle of beer.

"You mean hell, yeah," Benny corrects, raising the full shot glass in his hand.

"Hell, yeah," I echo, a beer *and* a shot on the table in front of me. "And just so we're clear," I add. "Tomorrow we give up the booze and the women. Tomorrow we start training for real."

The boys agree, and we drink to our plan.

Yeah, tomorrow we'll do all those things…

Read the rest of DESTINY ON ICE now:
Amazon: http://amzn.to/2gL1XC9